SWITCHED
AT BIRTH

SWITCHED AT BIRTH

The True Story of a Mother's Journey

Kathryn Kennish

Based on the ABC Family series
created by Lizzy Weiss

HYPERION

NEW YORK

791.4572
KEN

ISBN 978-1-4013-1275-6

Hyperion books are available for special promotions and
premiums. For details contact the HarperCollins Special
Markets Department in the New York office at 212-207-7528,
fax 212-207-7222, or email spsales@harpercollins.com.

FIRST PRINT EDITION

10   9   8   7   6   5   4

SUSTAINABLE FORESTRY INITIATIVE   Certified Sourcing
www.sfiprogram.org
SFI-00993

THIS LABEL APPLIES TO TEXT STOCK

We try to produce the most beautiful books possible, and we are
also extremely concerned about the impact of our manufacturing
process on the forests of the world and the environment as a whole.
Accordingly, we've made sure that all of the paper we use has been
certified as coming from forests that are managed, to ensure the
protection of the people and wildlife dependent upon them.

To all the people who have given me hope
and guidance on this journey, especially my family—
John, Toby, Bay, Daphne, Regina, and Adrianna.

SWITCHED
AT BIRTH

PROLOGUE

When I sat down to begin this book, to tell my story to the world, I thought that I would write about how a family was turned upside down and still managed to land on its feet.

To a large extent, that's what I have done. But in the process, I've discovered that landing on our feet was only the first test. The real trick is going to be staying there.

The people you will meet in this humble memoir of mine—my husband John, my daughter Bay, my other daughter Daphne, my son Toby, and Daphne's mother Regina (to name only the main players)—are in danger every day of losing the very precarious footing we've established. Imagine turning cartwheels during an earthquake—that's what we were up against, what we continue to be up against, and sometimes it seems like the aftershocks will go right on shaking us for the rest of our lives.

But we haven't given up yet, and I think that says a lot about us. But not all.

So in the following pages I will reveal to you the events and the emotions, the accidents, the errors in judgment, and I will endeavor to explain to you how these moments have defined who we are and the paths we have taken. I think you will all relate to the challenges I've faced, even if your children weren't switched at birth.

And if, by some chance, they were, then this is definitely the book for you.

I may not have *the* answers, but I do have *my* answers, and if mine can, in some small way, help lead you to your own, then I've accomplished what I've set out to do.

This book contains my advice for those who find themselves doing cartwheels in an earthquake, turning somersaults in a storm. Sooner or later you *will* land on your feet. And when you do, stand strong.

I promise you, you'll make it.

Kathryn Kennish

CHAPTER ONE

You marry a man—not just *a* man, but your dream man—and together, you plan things. Like where you will live, the kind of carpet you'll have in the family room, how you'll invest your money. But most of all, you plan your family. The word itself, when you finally find the courage to say it out loud, is nothing short of magical. At first you concern yourself with the practical things, like whether or not you're financially prepared for such a life-altering undertaking. But once you've decided you're ready, you begin to imagine in a million different ways the children you will bring into the world. You find yourselves whispering names to each other, trying them out to see how they will sound when cheered at the top of your lungs from the bleachers at the big football game. Or when announced over the PA system at the commencement ceremony of some Ivy League school. You wander into the baby furniture store and tell the clerk you're just looking, but the truth is, you already know exactly which crib you want, and exactly where it will be placed in that big, sunny room at the end of the upstairs hall.

And after the planning comes the wondering: Will our baby have my eyes? Will she have my husband's gift for sports? My love of anything chocolate?

You plan, and you dream, and you hope and you wonder. And then one day, after the longest (and somehow, shortest) nine months of your life, you get to take part in a miracle. It's a blur of pain (which you promptly forget) and joy (which you remember forever). And then, suddenly you're cradling a tiny bundle in your arms.

Your daughter.

You feel overwhelmed and overjoyed at the same time. And now you're *wondering* again: Is she warm enough? Am I holding her too tightly? Has my husband installed the car seat exactly as described in the instruction manual? He has, of course, because you made him go over the diagram a thousand times, but still, you wonder. . . .

You wonder if you have enough diapers waiting at home; you wonder how her big brother will react when he sees her for the first time; you wonder if she will be a good sleeper, a fussy eater, colicky, calm? Will she be musical, artistic, athletic?

But the one thing you absolutely do *not* wonder . . . not for one moment, not even for a single heartbeat, as this tiny, precious baby girl clutches your thumb and gazes up at you with absolute unconditional trust . . . the one thing you do not wonder is if she is *yours*.

Perhaps somewhere, someone has done the research, has calculated the precise odds of a newborn child in the United States of America accidentally being given to the wrong parents. I suspect the likelihood is similar to the chances of a person being struck by lightning. Virtually nonexistent. A near impossibility.

Well, this is my story—the story of me and my daughter, of my husband and my son and of two perfect strangers. It is the story of how one day, sixteen years ago, without notice, without warning, we were all struck by lightning.

* * *

It began with, of all things, a science project.

My daughter—my beautiful, dark-eyed, raven-haired daughter, Bay—had discovered through a lab experiment in science class, that her blood type was AB. For most people, being AB would be considered rare. For Bay, the daughter of two type A parents, it was genetically impossible. Naturally, my husband John and I simply chalked it up to an error, a mistake. Bay wasn't a kid with a particular gift for science after all; she was an artist. A great kid, a smart kid, but to our everlasting frustration, a kid to whom school was not a top priority. Which was why John and I were so easily inclined to shrug off her AB findings as merely Bay not giving the work her full attention. Obviously, she had misinterpreted the data.

But Bay felt differently. She was, if not freaked out exactly, troubled by the results. On our drive to school that morning—after Bay revealed the news about her blood type at breakfast—she reminded me, not unkindly, that she and I had almost nothing in common. Then I reminded *her* that this was due to the fact that she was a teenager and therefore if she did have anything in common with me, she'd be laughed right out of high school.

Maybe it was at this point that some tiny seed of panic began to form deep, deep within me. I don't know now, and I may never know. If I did feel something, I do know that I ignored it. If I sensed it—some small, gnawing sense that perhaps, just perhaps, something really wasn't adding up—I tamped it down.

Denial? Maybe.

Terror? More likely.

Because I was happy. *We* were happy. The Kennishes were happy and *whole*, and we would always be exactly as we were, as we'd always been.

God, how wrong I was.

As we drove toward school, Bay went on to muse over the fact that her coloring and her body type were nothing at all like mine. And then she admitted, haltingly, in a tone I'm sure she'd meant to sound indifferent but that to a mother's knowing ear echoed with deep curiosity and no small amount of worry, that she'd been teased more than once about being adopted.

That nearly floored me. *Adopted.* It was not a bad word, of course. It was a lovely word. It just wasn't a word I'd ever had cause to apply to my family. Our family. I gave birth to two beautiful, healthy children—Toby and Bay. I held them seconds after they were born, nursed them, loved them. And as I jokingly told my daughter that morning, "I'll show you my stretch marks."

I remember she didn't laugh.

"So we don't look alike," I conceded. I explained to Bay that as evidence went, this meant nothing. I, a strawberry blonde, had always taken a *vive la différence* stance when it came to the physical attributes of my little girl. I loved her glossy black hair and envied the way it tended to curl— unlike mine, which required boatloads of product to muster so much as a wave. I'd always bragged that her deep, dark chocolate eyes were her most beautiful feature. And I told her what I'd always believed—that her skin tone and dramatic hair color were attributes passed down to her from my Italian grandmother.

But Bay still seemed bothered by the whole AB thing.

So, thinking almost nothing of it, John and I agreed to put her concerns to rest by taking a blood test—a real one, the kind that goes beyond a high school science experiment. We agreed to the test for the same reason that we agreed to let her decorate her room in the style of Jackson Pollock when she was eight years old—because it really didn't seem like a big deal to us, but it did matter an awful lot to her.

So we said, "Sure. We'll take the test."

In the case of Jackson Pollock, let's just say that John and I were mildly shocked to walk into Bay's bedroom and find not only the walls but the floor, the curtains, the bedspread, and Bay herself splattered with splotches of bright red, blue, and yellow paint.

In the case of the blood test, the shock level went way beyond mild.

Because the follow-up testing, to which John and I had so casually, carelessly agreed, proved something that neither I nor my husband would have ever imagined.

It proved something that Bay had secretly feared, as it turns out, since long before she'd ever set foot in that science class, and it proved it conclusively. Irrefutably.

It proved that she wasn't ours.

Let me say that again, because it bears repeating. God knows, I repeated it myself a million times in those first few days after we found out. I repeated it out loud, and in whispers; I hissed it through gritted teeth and howled it on the heels of heart-wrenching sobs. According to John, I even mumbled it on more than one occasion while thrashing around in my sleep:

Bay. Wasn't. Ours.

The test proved it. The daughter I had loved, admired, fretted over, scolded, hugged, nagged, and adored for sixteen years had absolutely no biological connection to me, or to my husband, or to our son. It was unthinkable. Unspeakable. But it was true.

So here is some advice: If your children, like mine, ever complain to you that what they're learning in school is a bunch of irrelevant stuff that they'll never use "in real life," well, you can tell your kids for me that they are wrong.

Flat-out wrong.

Because what my daughter learned in school that day went way beyond relevant. And as far as "real life" is concerned, not only did this information apply directly and profoundly to our real lives, it actually redefined them.

The baby girl I had brought home from the hospital and placed gently in that crib in the big sunny room at the end of the upstairs hall was not the baby girl to whom I had given birth.

For a long time after the switch was revealed, people would ask me how I was dealing with it.

They would ask me that question in a tone that was part compassion, part fascination.

How are you dealing with it? they wanted to know.

Sometimes I actually had to try not to laugh. Sometimes I had to stop myself from grabbing them by the shoulders and shaking them, while screaming into their faces, "How do you *think* I'm dealing with it?"

But I knew they couldn't even begin to guess.

No one—no mother, no father, and no daughter—could ever imagine what this experience has been like for us.

Well, that's not entirely correct.

Regina and Daphne know, too.

* * *

We live in a town called Mission Hills, Kansas, a suburb of Kansas City, Missouri. It's nice.

Okay, I'm downplaying that. Mission Hills is much better than nice. It's not unusual to see homes priced at upward of ten million dollars. I'm not bragging. I'm just trying to create a sense of where I live, and, if I'm going to be brutally honest (and what is the point of writing a memoir if not brutal honesty?), who I am.

I am a Mission Hills mom. And that means, among other things, that I live comfortably. Very comfortably. But unlike other places in the world where money translates to shallow people competing in a consumerism free-for-all, Mission Hills, for me at least, still has the feeling of a small, family-oriented town. Midwestern values die hard here, and I like that. In Mission Hills, neighbors are not just people with whom you engage in a property dispute because their new clay tennis court is three millimeters too close to your new infinity pool. Corny as it may sound, there is still a sense of community here. Are we perfect? No, far from it. And I don't mean to imply that Mission Hills exists in a time warp, a *Little House on the Prairie*–meets–*The Waltons*–meets–*Father Knows Best* world where everyone spends all of their time pruning the azaleas and baking apple cobbler for the church bazaar. We have our problems, as you will see. Our kids act out and get grounded, our friends act out and get divorced. We make our share of mistakes here, just like anywhere else. But for the most part Mission

Hills is a wonderful place and I'm proud to call it home. The two minutes it takes to say grace before a special meal, to me, is time well spent, especially when there is so much to be thankful for.

For close to eighteen years now, I have been a Mission Hills mom, and for me, the significance of the "Mission Hills" part runs a distant second to the "Mom" part. I work hard to make my home feel warm and inviting; I have been careful to create a safe place for my children to thrive and grow, a place where they will always feel free to be themselves, without fear of disappointing us. It does not mean I am less capable than a so-called "working Mom." It just means I made a choice. I love what I do. And I know that I am lucky—no, not lucky, blessed—to have the life I have. Should I apologize for it? I don't think so, and besides that's a topic for someone else's memoir.

Because my kid was switched at birth. Try having *that* conversation during carpool on the way to soccer practice!

* * *

When a crisis occurs, people talk about reality speeding up and slowing down at the same time. They talk about how everything seems to happen in some kind of haze or blur. I used to think that was all just a big exaggeration. Now I know better.

John, Bay, and I met the genetic counselor in her office at the medical center. It was an ordinary office—pleasant, clean, with a big desk, and diplomas on the wall . . . and in this case there was the bonus of a funky plastic model of a double helix DNA molecule on the bookshelf. Bay, my artist, got a kick out of that. I wasn't in a "kicky" kind of mood.

John was quiet. I noticed him staring at the diplomas, and I knew he was trying to determine, based on the name of whatever institute of higher learning was imprinted there in gilt calligraphy letters, just exactly how qualified this genetic counselor would turn out to be. After twenty-two years of marriage I know how he thinks: *If that diploma is from Johns Hopkins or Stanford, then this woman knows her stuff and whatever she tells us will be right, accurate, true. If, on the other hand, she graduated from some lesser university or, worse, earned her degree in nine short weeks through some Internet pseudo-college . . . well, then whatever information she hits us with will be suspect and we'll have to go elsewhere to determine the future course of our lives.*

I peered at the diploma: Washington University in St. Louis. We were safe.

Or not.

I leaned back against the nubby fabric of the standard-issue office chair, remembering the last time I waited in a room like this. That time, John and I were holding hands, and our hearts were pounding just as rapidly as they were now. We were waiting for my ob-gyn to breeze in, with a chart in her hand, ready to tell me that the miscarriage hadn't done any permanent damage after all, ready to tell me that I was once again pregnant. This time, with Bay.

It was a beautiful memory.

But I didn't get to savor it for long. Because in the next moment, the genetic counselor, that bright, capable Washington U alum, came in with her file folder and sat behind her desk, and I knew from the expression on her face that this was going to be a very different conversation than the one sixteen years ago when the doctor smiled and handed me my prenatal vitamins.

Bay took my hand and I took John's. My right hand held Bay's gently, but with my left, I was squeezing John's fingers in a death grip, because I realized that this was the point when everything was about to get blurry.

I remember the counselor said, "mix-up." She said "ID anklets." I think Bay said something like, "I find my real parents and you find your real daughter," and even from deep within that horrible blur I thought my heart would shatter. I wanted to shout, "You *are* my real daughter, kiddo, and I have the aforementioned ID anklet tucked away in your baby book to prove it."

Then Bay whispered, "I knew it." To her credit, she did not turn to me with that familiar teenage smirk and say, "*I told you so*"; to my distress, she didn't turn to me at all.

As I sat there willing myself to breathe (because somehow I understood that dropping dead there in that cheerful little office wouldn't solve anything), I glanced at John. His jaw, that ruggedly handsome jaw with the tiniest shadow of afternoon scruff, was set so tight I thought he had turned to stone.

Again, I found myself reading his thoughts, and I knew that with every ounce of his being he was wishing that the genetic counselor's handsomely framed diploma had, in fact, come from BE-A-DOC.com after all. Because then maybe we would have had grounds to challenge her findings.

But I am a Midwestern girl, born and bred, and I know that Washington University doesn't churn out idiots.

So this . . . *this* . . . was real. This was happening. This crisis, this earthquake, this catastrophe of immeasurable proportions was really and truly happening. And it was happening exactly like they say it will happen—in that proverbial hazy blur, fast and slow at the same time. It was happening exactly like a crisis was supposed to happen.

But this time, it was happening to us.

* * *

Somehow, we made it home from the medical center. Somehow, John didn't drive off the road, and I didn't faint, and Bay didn't cry. I don't know how we got home, really, but somehow we did.

We didn't speak a single word on that ride, lost as we all were in our own thoughts. I noticed in the rearview that Bay was staring out the window, and I couldn't suppress the ridiculous feeling that she was searching the sidewalks and parks and crosswalks for her real—oops, *we say biological* (as though a formal parlance existed for this sort of thing, as if we were wording wedding invitations!)—family, whom she was bound to spot just around the next bend, at which time she would open the car door and leap out of the SUV to join them. I had a sickeningly vivid image of my daughter waving good-bye and heading off with these DNA-appropriate strangers to the life she was supposed to have lived, while her father and I sat helplessly, idling at a traffic light. I actually felt my index finger hovering above the button on the armrest that would engage the rear door's child-safety lock feature.

Hah! Talk about a day late and a dollar short!

I jerked my hand away from the button and squeezed my eyes shut tight. I was only ten minutes into this nightmare and already I was teetering on the brink of insanity!

When I'd successfully forced aside the picture of Bay flinging herself from the vehicle, I made myself focus on those final minutes of our meeting with the genetic counselor. John's last question to her was "Where is the other baby?" (He'd said "other," not "our," and I don't know if this was for Bay's benefit or simply because at that point he couldn't bring himself to think of this absent child as anything other than "other.") The counselor informed us that she had already put in a call to the hospital's legal department, and as soon as we left, she would begin the arduous process of reviewing the maternity records for October 22, 1995.

So she would assist us in finding our misplaced child. Were we supposed to be grateful? Did she expect me to compliment her on her work ethic? What I wanted to know was: Where was this conscientious professionalism sixteen years ago?

"Well," I said, standing (still holding Bay's hand) and giving the counselor a steady look. "We will leave you to it, then. And please do notify us the minute you find what you're looking for."

What she was looking for was my daughter, but I didn't see the point in mentioning that. Instead, I turned away from her and her Washington University credentials and left the office.

And now here we were, pulling into the winding drive of our stately Tudor home, on its four lushly manicured acres of prime, secluded real estate. In the distance, I could hear the sound of a lawn mower, and the clean smell of newly cut grass made the world seem somehow innocent and fresh. I could see the house now, and I knew that inside everything was orderly and in its rightful place. My kitchen calendar was marked with dentist visits and bake sale dates and a mother-daughter manicure appointment (Bay would choose black nail polish as always, but I was okay with that). John's Royals jersey was hanging in its shadow-box frame in the basement game room, and the first of Toby's potential college brochures was tacked to the bulletin board beside the fridge, sharing a thumbtack with the recipe for edamame salad I'd recently clipped from *Better Homes and Gardens*.

I don't need to tell you what wasn't in that house, in its rightful place. I think this was the first time I truly understood that it is possible to have everything—*everything*—you'd ever hoped for and still feel utterly and completely bereft.

As John guided the SUV into the garage bay, I sent up a silent prayer imploring heaven: *Find her*. And then, before I got out of the car, I imagined myself sending a telepathic communiqué directly to the genetic counselor. Presumably she would be barricaded in her office by now, doggedly poring over every medical record, insurance form, and birth certificate she could get her hands on. The words of my message were the same as the ones of my prayer—*Find her*. But this time they sounded more like a command.

Find her. Find my baby!

Then John was opening the car door for me and offering his hand.

It was time to tell Toby.

* * *

We called him into the kitchen, and John and I stood on one side of the marble-topped island, while Toby stood beside Bay on the other. She kept her eyes low, studying the veins that swirled through the marble as though she had never seen them before, and I think this was her brother's first clue that something was not right. His little sister was being quiet. That never happened.

John was staring out the window above the sink. Also silent.

So it fell to me to do the talking. It fell to me to inform my son that his life was about to change irrevocably, and forever.

I explained everything. Calmly, and in the exact same scientific terminology the counselor had used.

At first, Toby, my sweet, musically gifted son who has my honey-colored hair and his father's broad shoulders, thought we were kidding.

I said, "Toby, sweetheart. Do you really think we would kid about this?"

I looked at Bay, still tracing the silvery web of capillaries eternally captured inside the shimmering stone of the countertop. She was biting her lip. Waiting.

I wondered if she was remembering the time when her brother was nine and she was seven and he taped a crayon-lettered "BAY KEEP OUT" sign on his bedroom door. Or how he'd teased her relentlessly four years later, after finding the notebook in which she'd doodled three pages worth of *Mrs. Bay Timberlake, Bay Kennish-Timberlake*, and *Bay loves Justin*.

I wondered if Toby was remembering that, too.

But if I was hoping for a warm and fuzzy moment, a scene straight out of a Hallmark card commercial, I sure as heck didn't get it. Toby, laid-back future rock star that he was, simply shrugged and said, "Okay."

Okay? Now he was the one who had to be kidding. This was a revelation, and he was acting like I'd just informed him we were having lamb chops for dinner! I swung my gaze to Bay, expecting her to feel crushed at this lack of emotion, but when she looked up from the countertop, she was smiling.

"Yeah, okay," she said.

John and I looked at each other, and I'm happy to say he was as baffled by this reaction as I was. Once again we were lost in teen world, and we didn't have the guidebook.

"Oh, and by the way," Toby said, reaching into the fruit bowl for a red delicious. "Can you get those paint cans out of the driveway? I nearly broke my neck on them when I was carrying my amp into the studio."

"Too bad you didn't break the amp," Bay tossed out in her famous deadpan tone. "That would have put us all out of our misery."

And that was that.

Or so I thought.

But I was soon to discover that my children could surprise me in ways I'd never dreamed.

CHAPTER TWO

John wanted to kill somebody.

Anybody.

Maybe everybody.

He was letting his anger take over, as though being angry would be easier for him than this sickening cocktail of confusion, devastation, and heartbreak. What he wanted was to *blame* somebody.

That night, we told the kids we were exhausted and just wanted to turn in. But we lied. I knew we weren't going to be sleeping at all that night. For all I knew, I might never sleep again.

I watched as my husband paced around our bedroom; he moved like the athlete he was, in long strides, with an easy, masculine grace. He looked like an athlete is supposed to look: ready to fight, ready to win. But this wasn't a game. The stakes were too high.

What John wanted was to see justice served. He wanted to make somebody pay. And I suppose I saw his point.

But right then, I wasn't thinking about retribution.

I was thinking about Bay.

Bay, the teenage girl down the hall, sleeping in her room in her big bed under the Frida Kahlo quote stenciled on her wall.

And the other Bay, the infant I held only once, when she was still bloody and screaming from the doctor's slap on her backside. Where was *she*? Where was *her* room? Would I ever know? Did I even want to?

"I'm going to call Harrison Burke," John said, grabbing the phone. "He'll know how to handle this."

"Harrison represents professional athletes," I reminded him. Harrison had been John's attorney since his Kansas City Royals days. He was a brilliant, and intimidating, man, but I wasn't sure this situation fell into his area of expertise. "We aren't negotiating an endorsement deal with a sneaker company. And besides, you can't call anyone now, it's after midnight."

Calmly, I took the cordless receiver out of his hand. It was the fourth time I'd taken the phone away from him since we'd closed the bedroom door behind us. In that short span of time he had threatened to call the *Kansas City Herald* and demand they do an exposé on the hospital. He'd dialed the first six digits of the local police precinct before he realized that as far as we knew no actual crime had been committed. He wanted to call the FBI or the CIA and put out an APB on a missing girl who was born Bay Madeline Kennish in October of 1995 and now, sixteen years later, could be anywhere—*anywhere*—in the whole wide world.

"What about Aaron Silvers, then? I'll call Aaron. He might know—"

Aaron was a personal injury lawyer we knew from the tennis club. I may not have been a legal genius, but I did know that this situation went way beyond personal injury.

He reached for the phone again, but I intercepted.

"It's after midnight," I repeated. "You can call Aaron in the morning."

For a second, John looked like he might lunge for the phone again, but he surprised me by sinking down onto the bed. The scruff I'd noticed on his chin in the genetic counselor's office was darker now, and his eyes looked tired.

"Why?" he asked in a hollow voice. "Why did this happen?" He covered his face with his hands and asked the question again. "*Why?*"

And suddenly I was reeling back in time to when Bay was little. Whenever she'd ask me for something that I, in my maternal wisdom, did not see fit to provide—a Popsicle right before dinner, permission to swim during a thunderstorm— naturally I would say no.

Then she would ask, "Why?"

And I'd say, "Because."

The reason for my succinct reply was that after a long day of baking cupcakes for the teacher appreciation luncheon or helping Toby rig up his model of the solar system for the science fair (the neighbor's dog had eaten Saturn, a major setback), I just didn't have it in me to explain to my precocious four-year-old *why* a sugary snack would spoil her dinner, or *why*, given the fact that water and lightning are a deadly combination, she needed to get out of the pool and come into the house *immediately* without doing one last cannonball off the diving board.

As far as I was concerned, "Because" was a perfectly acceptable response.

But, of course, Bay would persist. She'd scrunch up her angelic little face and demand to know, "Because *why*?"

And with my hands planted firmly on my hips, and my own face as stern as any marine drill sergeant's, I'd state

(Moms, you know where this is going, right?): "Because *I'm* the mommy, *that's* why!"

Bay didn't always like it, but that's where the conversation about "why" would grind to a halt. And then I'd be free to go back to frosting cupcakes or positioning Toby's Mercury in its proper place in our little mock heaven.

But now my husband—the strongest, most confident man I knew, a man used to having more answers than questions—was asking me why. *Why* was he suddenly in need of legal advice in the middle of the night? *Why* was someone telling us that the beautiful young woman we had loved for every second of every minute of every day of the last sixteen years did not belong to us?

"*Why, Kathryn? Why?*"

In lieu of an answer (which I didn't have then and still don't have now), I wrapped my arms around him and held him close. He was aching inside. He had no idea how to protect us from this, and protecting us was his reason for living.

He sat there on the edge of the bed with his head in his hands, and the room went still. He didn't move, he didn't speak, he didn't cry. He just sat there and let the pain have its moment.

I, on the other hand, wanted to sob. I wanted to give over to the pain and dissolve into tears. Instead I drew my husband closer and held on tighter. Tonight would be his turn; my turn would come soon enough, and, I suspected, it would come with a vengeance. But tonight I would be the one to stay strong, to keep it together, to protect him, to protect Bay, to protect us all.

Why?

Because I'm the mommy, that's why.

❈ ❈ ❈

Around three that morning (because I couldn't even close my eyes to rest, let alone sleep) I was bringing an armful of freshly folded towels up to the hall bath, two doors down from Bay's bedroom. Some people, when they're anxious or overwrought, do crossword puzzles, or read the Bible, or hop on the elliptical; *I* do laundry. And I'm glad, because if I'd been downstairs feeling the burn, or pondering a five-letter word for "large waterfowl," I would have missed it.

Toby was in Bay's room. They were talking. At three in the morning.

I didn't panic. I'd gotten used to the vampire-esque nocturnal habits of teenagers long ago and assumed Toby had merely wandered in to borrow her calculator or show her some idiotic video on YouTube. I was sure it was no big deal. Still, I did what any other mother worth her salt would do in such circumstances:

I tiptoed away in the opposite direction to give my beloved young adults their rightful privacy. . . .

Um, *no.* I absolutely did *not* do that, and if you believed for one millisecond that I did, then you are not yet the mother of teenagers. Because in certain situations, eavesdropping is utterly permissible, even advised. (Refer back to the "I'm the Mommy" clause, above, for clarification.)

First, I quickly deposited my neatly folded towels in the linen closet, then I flattened myself against the wall and crept quietly in the direction of Bay's slightly open door.

I could tell from the occasional metallic creak that Toby

was sitting in Bay's wicker swing, swaying slowly back and forth.

"Let's be real," he was saying. "Nobody was buying Mom's Italian grandmother story."

"Yeah," Bay agreed. "I always knew that was a pretty feeble explanation. I was just so thrilled that I'd escaped the ginger curse, I never bothered to question it. You on the other hand . . . I'm sorry but that whole Ron Weasley vibe you've got going on must seriously suck."

There was a muffled *whumpfh*, and I guessed that Toby had probably flung a pillow across the room, no doubt aiming for her head.

I figured that friendly fire marked the end of the conversation, and I was just about to head back downstairs to start hand-washing some delicates when Bay said, "It's weird, isn't it? That we don't share any DNA."

"Oh, please. Like you ever shared anything! You *always* took the last ice cream sandwich, you *never* let me have a single prize from fifteen years' worth of cereal boxes, and the only time I ever got to ride shotgun in my whole life was that summer you busted your ankle and had to ride in the back with your cast up on the seat. So why would I expect anything different when it comes to chromosomes? You, little sister, are not a sharer."

"That's very true." It got quiet for a moment. Then Bay said, "What about the little sister part?"

"What about it?"

"Am I . . . I mean, ya know . . . do you still think of me as . . . *that*? As your little sister?"

In the hallway, I held my breath.

"Duh. How else would I think of you?"

"I dunno." I could picture Bay's face—she would be giving him her "I'm acting like I don't care, but really, I do" expression. "As a stranger. An interloper."

"*Interloper.* Ooh. Good word."

"Yeah. I go to prep school, remember?" She sighed. "It's just that this whole thing is, like, so *freaky.* So maybe now . . . *I'm* freaky."

"You've always been freaky."

"Shut up!" I could hear the smile in her voice. "I'm serious, Toby."

"So am I." The swing creaked louder, which I think meant he'd stood up and was walking toward her. "Bay, listen, I honestly don't care about some stupid 'switched at birth' thing."

I closed my eyes and pressed myself against the wall. *Some stupid switched at birth thing.* If only it were that simple.

"You're still my sister. You always will be. Hell, I came to terms with that punishment a long time ago." There was a pause in which I imagined him quirking an eyebrow in pretend thought. "Although, I don't suppose there's any chance this kid they switched you with could be a boy? 'Cause a brother would be a major upgrade. . . ."

"You do know that I *will* kill you, right?" (I knew Bay was narrowing her eyes at him, giving him her trademark smirk.) "With all this 'extreme emotional distress' I'm currently experiencing, there's not a jury in the world that would convict me!"

"You're my sister," Toby said again. "We've got history. I'm used to you."

Bay let out her breath in a long rush. "So it's not gonna be creepy and miserable around here, then?"

"Not any more than it's ever been before," Toby answered without missing a beat.

They laughed, and it was a sound I recognized in my heart: My two children laughing . . . together.

I figured I'd pushed my luck far enough, and if I didn't go then, I'd blow my cover. So I left, with the sound of their collective laughter lingering in my ears.

I don't really know what else they talked about that night, but I like to think that maybe Toby offered Bay a hug, and Bay—the little girl who once dreamed of being Mrs. Justin Timberlake—accepted it gladly. Of course, when the hug ended, she probably said something like "Dude, can you please get over the spiky hair thing, 'cause you almost just blinded me with your bangs."

To which Toby would have replied, "Jealous, Morticia?"

But it doesn't matter what they said. It's what they *felt*. And that in their own way, in their unique, clever brother-sister shorthand, they were working it out. It would get weirder, I knew that, and it would take time until we all understood this new world of ours. If that was even possible. At the time, I didn't know.

But I did know this: Thanks to two amazing kids and a freshly laundered load of whites, I'd gotten my Hallmark fix.

It's funny how the darkest moments of your life can bring about the best ones.

* * *

In the morning, John did call Harrison Burke, but when push came to shove he couldn't bring himself to tell the elderly attorney, who had seen him through the complicated legal dealings of professional sports, what had happened.

He merely hinted to Harry that we might be needing his services in the near future and got off the phone as fast as he could.

And that was when I realized that somewhere in the last twenty-four hours a decision had been made: This was a secret. A secret with a capital S. A secret that we, as a family, would attempt to keep out of circulation for as long as we could. Our town is not known for the kind of mean-spirited gossip that perhaps other affluent communities are subject to, but I understood that it was simply human nature to find fascination in a story like this, and I suspected even the kindest-hearted citizens of Mission Hills would be curious at the very least.

The thing was, it wasn't a "story"; it was our *life*.

And for moment at least, I did not want anyone to know. Not the neighbors, not the people at Bay's school. No one would be told but the strangers who could help us untangle this web—lawyers and private investigators and whatever other bonded professionals were called in to handle situations like this. In fact, I decided that at this point it would be best not even to tell my mother.

"*Especially* not your mother," John agreed. We both knew that my mother (who lived in that rarified world reserved for women who married exceptionally well the second time around) would provide a great deal of opinion on the topic, but that none of her suggestions would be particularly helpful.

Over the last several months, I've had time to consider this element of the journey, to ask myself why, at the beginning, it was imperative to me to keep the information to ourselves. What made me feel that this was something I'd take to the grave, if I could?

Yes, it was personal.

Yes, it was private.

But why was I so damn terrified of what would happen when people found out? Did I think they would laugh at us? Did I think they would pity us?

No.

What I thought was that they would judge us.

But we hadn't done anything wrong, it was a terrible, terrible mistake. An accident, one that was, as far as we could tell, utterly absent of malice. The switch was an exceedingly unfortunate twist of fate. But it wasn't a crime. It wasn't a scandal.

So why did I feel, at least in the beginning, that nobody could know?

I will give you the honest answer. The answer it has taken me months of take-no-prisoners introspection and soul-searching to arrive at. I will say it here, and it will hurt me even to put the words on paper, but this is a journey toward understanding, toward healing, and if I don't say it now, I may never. So here it is:

I felt ashamed.

I. Felt. Ashamed.

Ashamed, and embarrassed and stupid, because I had brought home the wrong child *and I didn't even know it.*

Neither did John, of course. But there is a difference. I was that child's mother. We shared a body for God's sake; I nourished her inside me for nine months, and when I pushed her into this world, I took her to my breast and fed her.

And then I lost her. *And I didn't even know it.*

Where were my instincts? Isn't the female of the species hardwired to recognize her own offspring? Isn't there a scent, an energy, a singing in the blood, a sharing of the soul? Or have we evolved away from even that most basic ability, that deepest of human connections?

I *failed*. I failed my daughter, and my family and myself. At least that's what I believed at the time—that's what I felt in my heart, in my bones, and in every atom of my body.

I failed to know my own child.

And I was ashamed.

* * *

The search for our biological daughter was, in the scheme of things, far easier than we'd ever anticipated. But that does not mean it was simple. Or quick. John and I wanted to do everything we could, but the hospital hit us with that impenetrable shield known as HIPAA, and with regard to official records we were granted access to absolutely nothing. There was also a good deal of bureaucratic posturing taking place, not to mention a fair amount of red tape.

But red tape is no match for green money.

John, who'd played third base for the Kansas City Royals, had spent most of his adult life literally "playing hardball," and this time was no exception. As a businessman, he immediately recognized that the only weapon we could hope to have in our arsenal was high-powered legal representation. Ultimately, John called Harry back, and Harry said that although trial law wasn't his specialty, he could at least get the ball rolling for us by throwing his considerable legal influence at the hospital on our behalf. What we needed at the moment was an attorney who was nothing short of a legal WMD, and Harrison Burke was definitely that. For one solid month, from behind his gleaming antique desk in his mahogany-paneled office, this soldier of the law earned his astronomical retainer by calling the hospital daily to issue demands and ultimatums. When that failed to produce results, he would drop by in person with promises of hellfire if the search for our child was not handled expeditiously and with every resource the hospital had at its disposal.

And what did John and I do?

We spent a small fortune on legal fees.

And we waited.

* * *

There are things about those weeks that I really don't remember. I think it must have been some involuntary coping mechanism kicking in, because there are entire days of which I have no recollection whatsoever. I know I drove Bay to school. I'm certain I prepared meals. I got the mail and made the coffee. I ate (although not a lot and with very little enjoyment). I breathed. I prayed.

Other things, I was less diligent about: my cuticles; the geraniums in the planter boxes on the patio; answering the phone (unless Caller ID told me it was our secret weapon of an attorney checking in). I skipped PTA meetings. I forgot about lipstick entirely.

I also spent a lot of time alone in the master suite with the door shut, flipping through the bulky photo albums I'd compiled during my brief but zealous "scrapbooking" phase. I would stare at snapshots (remember: my kids were born in an era when pictures existed on film rather than in cyberspace) of Bay as a baby, a toddler, a toothless first-grader, a fourth-grade Halloween princess. I'd run my fingers over them, as if to prove that they were real, that the memories captured there on those shiny, four- by six-inch rectangles had actually occurred.

When Bay was at school, I'd go into her room, telling myself I was there to dust the furniture or Windex the mirrors. I happen to be one of a very few women in my particular demographic who opt to clean their own houses. I'm sure there are a zillion psychological explanations that could be offered as to why I choose to vacuum my own carpets and scrub my own toilets, but the real reason is simply this: Nobody, and I mean *nobody*, would ever clean my house as well as I clean it myself.

Well, maybe my mother. But that's another chapter.

The point is, I learned about housekeeping at the hands of the master, Bonnie Tamblyn Dixon, and no cleaning lady or maintenance staff I might hire could ever meet my expectations when it comes to scouring the kitchen sink or keeping the vegetable bin free of mold. So, yes, I clean my own house.

But in the course of those six weeks, as I waited to hear something, *anything*, regarding the whereabouts of my biological daughter, I will admit that I did very little cleaning at all. When I wandered into Bay's room, as I said, it was ostensibly to pair up her school socks (Bonnie folds, I roll) or collect the empty glasses from the nightstand, but what I really did was sink into the soft comforter on her bed and just look around.

I'd see the random snatches of artwork-in-progress on a page of an open sketchbook; I would marvel at the way she'd arranged her perfume bottles on the dresser (she's a big fan of the Ed Hardy fragrances). I'd pull her pillow to my face and just breathe in the scent of her shampoo and makeup remover lingering there, as if I could breathe Bay herself into my lungs.

What would my life have been like if she hadn't been here?

It was a sickening thought, and I felt tears welling in my eyes every time it forced itself into my mind, but still, I couldn't help but wonder. Without my Bay—not the one I conceived, but the one I *received*—who would I be?

Her quirks, her fears, her talents, her sense of humor, her *Bay-ness* had contributed to my maternal evolution and informed my sense of motherhood from the day we brought her home. Toby did, too, of course, but his contribution was different, as every child's is bound to be. With Toby I learned how to mother a child who approached the world with caution; with Bay I had to shift gears and learn to mother a kid who barreled into everything at ninety miles an hour, oblivious to danger and utterly opposed to anything conventional. Toby taught me patience, but Bay taught me to embrace the unexpected.

And believe me, the irony of *that* is not lost on me at all.

The point is, instead of cleaning, I sat on Bay's bed and tried to picture a Kennish family that did not include her.

Impossible.

Then I'd stand beside her window and gaze out.

As though I were expecting to see a teenage girl I'd never met but would recognize on sight, just walking up the driveway.

As though I were expecting a miracle.

Which, in a way, I was.

And that's when the what-ifs would start. What if we never find her? What if the mother who took her home had moved out of the country and left no forwarding address? What if there had been an accident—anything could happen over the course of sixteen years, after all—a car wreck, a plane crash, a drowning? What if *that* mother hadn't watched and worried and planned and protected the way *I* would have—the way I *did* . . . for *her* daughter?

What if . . . ?

And the worst part was that I knew Bay's head was swirling with what-ifs, too. But every time I broached the subject, she'd crack a joke and turn the conversation in another direction. She wasn't ready, or perhaps wasn't able, to put her own what-ifs into words. For once, Bay was taking her time.

Then one day, she found me in her room, looking out the window.

"You're home early," I said, feeling foolish and embarrassed at being caught just standing there. I picked up the Windex bottle, but since I'd neglected to include paper towels in that day's cleaning charade it was a useless bluff.

"I'm not early," Bay informed me. "It's after four o'clock."

"Is it? Gee." *Time flies when you're waiting for your missing child to find you.* "How was school?"

"You know, school-ish." She gave me her wry smile. "On the upside, I ditched science class, so I didn't discover anything else that might potentially rip our family apart."

She dropped her backpack on the floor. Reflexively, I picked it up and put it on a chair.

"That's not what's happening, honey."

"Really?" Bay slipped out of her cherry-red school blazer, the one that goes so gorgeously with her porcelain complexion (it, too, landed on the floor). "Because you've been wandering around this house like a zombie for weeks."

"I've got a lot on my mind," I said vaguely.

"Like what you're going to do when the prodigal daughter returns?" She grinned. "See? And you thought I never paid attention in Sunday school."

I laughed.

"So instead of standing around here pretending to Windex stuff, shouldn't you be off planning the Welcome Home Whoever You Are extravaganza?" Bay frowned, feigning great concern. "What's the protocol for this sort of thing? Will it be a black tie event, maybe? Or more casual, like cocktails and finger food on the patio at dusk? And saliva swabs for everyone, ya know, in keeping with the theme."

"Good question." I responded with a grin of my own. "I guess I'll have to look it up. Maybe Emily Post has some insight on the etiquette for Whoever You Are parties."

"Excellent. Sounds like a plan." Bay picked up the sketch pad from her desk and began to doodle.

I watched her for a moment, thinking I'd leave her alone to work, but the lighthearted teasing had gone a long way toward lifting my spirits. Suddenly, I felt ready to say something I'd been meaning to say for days now.

"Bay . . ." I sat on the bed and waited for her to look up from her drawing. "I want you to know . . . I *need* you to know that no matter what happens, you are and always will be my daughter. The switch . . . it doesn't change anything."

"Actually . . ." A shadow flickered in her eyes. "It changes everything."

This hit me like a punch. "What do you mean?"

"I mean, I'm not related to you. I'm not your kid. And it's not even like I was adopted. If I was adopted, you would have picked me, you would have consciously chosen to bring me home and make me a part of your family. But you didn't. I just showed up. Like junk mail."

I actually smiled. "Did you seriously just compare yourself to junk mail?"

"Yes. And not the good kind, either."

"*Is* there a good kind?"

"I don't know, I guess I was thinking of catalogues. But definitely not J.Crew. . . ." She shook her head in a gesture of dismissal. "Wow, this conversation has gone off on a pretty strange tangent."

"A tangent! So you listened in geometry as well as Sunday school, huh?"

Bay shot me a sideways smile. "Why does everyone around here get such a shock out of me knowing things?"

"Hmmm, I dunno. Shall we talk about your last report card?"

"I'd rather not." Bay laughed, then surprised me by laying her head on my shoulder. Instantly, my arms went around her, and I knew that there was nothing on this earth that could get me to let go.

"You will always be my daughter," I said softly, against her hair. "You will always be *our* daughter, our little girl, our baby. Not adopted, not accidental, not junk mail."

I felt her relax beside me, felt the tension drain from her

shoulders. She snuggled closer to me and I squeezed her tighter.

"And you will never be my J.Crew catalogue," she said softly.

I took that for the compliment she'd intended it to be and laughed.

"You're stuck with me, kid," I whispered.

"Thank God," she whispered back.

CHAPTER THREE

Five weeks and three days after finding out that our Bay had come home with us by accident, the hospital spokesperson (a generic term if ever I heard one) called the house. It was 9:15 on a Tuesday morning; I remember because I should have been halfway to my Bikram yoga class by then. But I wasn't. The mood I'd been in for the last month hadn't exactly been conducive to outside activities. Absently, my hand went to the limp ponytail at my neck. When had I last washed my hair?

We took the call in John's den. He hit the button for speaker phone, and the counselor cut right to the chase.

"I have excellent news. We've found the other child."

My stomach reacted in much the same way that it had two years ago when Bay dragged me onto the Rock 'n' Rollercoaster at Disney World.

"Where is she?" I heard myself ask; my voice was shaking.

"Nearby, actually," the counselor reported. There was a note of triumph in her tone, as though this fortunate proximity was somehow her doing.

"And when can we . . . ," I swallowed hard, "meet her?" The thought of being introduced to my own child put me back on the roller coaster—dead center in the upside-down and backward loop, to be precise.

"Soon."

But I had been waiting and wondering for over a month, and soon did not sound soon enough for me.

"The hospital board will be meeting day after tomorrow to decide when you can—"

"Excuse me," John interrupted. "Are you telling me that the hospital board is going to tell me when I can meet my own daughter?"

"It's complicated, Mr. Kennish," the counselor explained.

Before John could reply to that, I cleared my throat. "Can you tell us where she is, at least? Where she lives, exactly?"

There was a pause, followed by an evasive answer. "Missouri."

Like "soon," this told us nothing.

Struggling to maintain his cool, John asked, "Can you narrow that down?"

Of course she could. But she wasn't about to.

"Nearby," the counselor repeated. "As I said, it's complicated. But we think . . . that is to say, we here at the hospital *feel* it would be best for all concerned if we keep that specific information to ourselves for the time being."

Did she actually think I gave a rat's patootie about how "they there at the hospital" *felt*? They there at the hospital were the ones who lost my daughter in the first place.

"This is ridiculous!" I shouted, leaning close to the speaker.

"I understand," she assured me. "But we feel it's for the best."

"Fine," John conceded with a roll of his eyes. "Just promise me you'll call us the minute the board adjourns."

"I will do that, sir. And thank you for your patience."

John punched the "off" button and gave me a look. "It's complicated," he mimicked dryly.

I was on my feet now, stomping around John's den, powered by pure adrenaline. "I can't believe they won't tell us where she lives! What do they think? That if they give us the address we're going to just show up and take her home with us? Spirit her away in the middle of the night?"

It occurred to me that that was probably exactly what they thought.

"Kathryn . . ." My husband leaned back in his desk chair, a bemused expression on his face. "She's nearby."

I stopped pacing. I nodded, smiled. "She's close," I whispered, and reached up to wipe the tears from my cheeks. "John . . ."

"Yes?"

"I have to wash my hair."

* * *

Ten minutes later, I was reveling in the silky sensation of shampoo in my hair. I had the shower head turned to "massage" and I'd let the water get extra hot, so the master bath was shrouded in a steamy mist.

It was in this dreamlike setting that I was hit with an incredible realization.

Somewhere—*nearby*—another mother had just received the same phone call I had.

Another mother had been told that her biological child had been located . . . which would likely seem exceedingly strange to her, since she hadn't even known her child was missing.

I recalled a formula I'd learned back in tenth-grade chemistry: *For every action there is an equal and opposite reaction.*

Now, somewhere nearby, a woman was waiting to meet Bay.

But then what? What would she expect? What would she be willing to give? And worse, what would she want to take?

Suddenly, the steamy cloud in my bathroom felt more like a cold, ominous fog, and even under the stream of hot water I felt a chill.

* * *

"Nearby" became the concept that consumed me. All I could think of was that if this child had been "nearby" all this time, maybe I'd seen her somewhere, maybe we'd crossed paths.

She could be living as close as the next town over. She could be as "nearby" as the next block. She could be living in the same school district! The girls had been born in the same hospital after all; evidently the family had stayed local, and there were only a handful of elementary schools in the area.

This thought had me searching my memory to recall if, over the course of Bay's elementary school years, there had ever been another little girl in her class or grade whose birthday was October 22, 1995. Did I remember any drama about overlapping party dates? Had another mother ever sent in celebratory peanut-free birthday treats to be passed out during snack time on the same day that I had? No, Bay assured me. She'd always been the only kid whose name

was block-lettered on the classroom birthday calendar for
October 22.

All right, then maybe my missing child and her mystery mom had visited the same kid-friendly places my children and I had frequented over the years. I might have passed right by my daughter at the farmer's market or sat beside her on the gym mat at Bay's Mommy and Me music class. Was there a chance that, at some point in the last decade and a half, this little girl and Bay had needed new undershirts or colored pencils or tennis shoes at the same time? If so, she could have been at the mall riding the down escalator at the exact same moment that Bay and I had been riding the up one. We could have glided right past each other on our opposite shopping trajectories and never even known it.

Had she been there, right before my very eyes and I'd missed her? Had I been close enough to touch her and blown my chance?

John told me it was silly to even think like that. If, by some incredible coincidence, by some utterly random accident, I had encountered our missing daughter, it wouldn't have mattered because I wouldn't have even known I should be looking.

I said, "Don't talk to me about incredible coincidences and random accidents, pal! I'm living in the eye of the storm of an incredibly coincidental random accident."

He laughed, and once again I understood that testosterone is a major obstacle to the creative thought process.

The only thing I can compare those weeks to was the way I had felt when I was pregnant. It is a time, as any mother knows, that is characterized chiefly by an overwhelming sense of anticipation and wonder. With both my kids, I'd firmly instructed the doctor to keep his ultrasound findings to himself so I could experience that old-school sensation of hearing him announce, after my final, heroic push: "It's a boy!" or "It's a girl!" I didn't care which, as long as the words "healthy and normal," followed closely thereafter. (This decision, by the way, irritated my mother to no end; she couldn't understand why I would forgo the benefits of current technology, especially since the information would have been so helpful to her in purchasing the layette.)

But I liked the idea of the baby's gender being the first news that he or she and I would hear together.

Anticipation, of course, has its downside. I tried not to listen to the "horror stories" of incompetent doctors, undetected congenital conditions, and errant umbilical cords. Because the truth is, although billions of women have billions of babies every single day, there is so much that can go wrong. So along with the pink-and-blue daydreams came the black-and-white nightmares—the panic, the worry, the knowledge that occasionally Mother Nature slipped up and this resulted in "complications."

But then John would come home at the end of the day and place a big, loud smackeroo in the center of my enormous belly, and I'd forget the fear and jump ahead to hope.

And in those hopeful moments (which far outnumbered the panicky ones), pregnancy reminded me of a poem I read in college by Emily Dickinson: "I dwell in Possibility." The whole world would be open for this little person I was carrying. I would tell myself, "He could be a surgeon; she could be president of the United States," and then I would laugh at how colloquial and old-fashioned those plans sounded. "He could be a rock star; she could be a ground-breaking artist."

All of these feelings were similar to the ones that soothed and assaulted me over those weeks of waiting to hear from the hospital. Just as I had as a young expectant mother, I was preparing to bring a new child into my family and into my heart.

Only this time, the child was going to be a full-fledged teenager, raised who-knows-where, by who-knew-whom.

So I didn't just dwell in possibility.

I also dwelled in abject terror.

* * *

This is a confession:

The next day, the hospital called again to set up the meeting. It would take place in three days, back in the genetic counselor's office where Part One of the "Switched at Birth" story had been told to us. The sequel would include two additional characters: my biological daughter and the woman who raised her.

I suspected they wanted to hold this meeting at the counselor's office because they didn't want what they feared could potentially become an unpleasant scene playing out on their turf, where anyone with a camera phone could make a bad situation worse. And by worse, I mean public.

I immediately called John at the car wash and told him. After that, like any well-organized Mission Hills mom, I wrote the date and time of this meeting on my kitchen calendar, and then I felt stupid because it was noted between the square where I'd written *change baking soda box in fridge* and the one that said, *book club*.

That night, I woke up holding a scream back in my throat.

My heart was racing. I was sweating and my hands shook as I slid out of bed and grabbed my bathrobe. I bit down hard on the shriek that was trying to release itself into the night.

"Call it off."

That is what the scream wanted to say. Those were the words it was made of, the words that would have shattered the silence of my sleeping house if I had only opened my mouth and let them.

"Call it off." I could call it off. I could cancel the meeting, tell the counselor, "Thank you anyway, but I've decided to keep my life. To keep my daughter all to myself. To let these enormously complicated bygones be bygones and go on as though nothing happened."

I ran barefoot down the hall and pushed opened Bay's bedroom door. She was, for once, not pulling a Facebook all-nighter. She was sleeping. Like a baby.

Like my baby.

I sat on the edge of the bed and shook her gently.

"Mom? What's wrong?"

"We can call it off," I whispered, taking her beautiful, sleepy face into my hands. "We don't have to do it, Bay, we don't have to. We can just call it all off."

She looked at me, lost somewhere between wakefulness and dreams, lost in two worlds, and she tried to make sense of what I was saying to her.

"You don't want to meet your biological daughter?"

No, it's your biological mother I don't want you to meet.
All I could manage in reply was a pathetic little shrug.

She sat up and gave a slow shake of her head. Her mass of onyx hair was a riotous tumble of glossy curls. Bay must have realized that I was trembling, because she tucked the blanket around me.

"We can call it off," I said again.

"We can," she agreed.

The night settled around us, like shards of broken glass, and I felt the silence cut me.

"But we can't," I said. "Can we?"

Bay shook her head.

Because to call it off, to change our minds and say, "You know what? Never mind. We're just going to pretend this never happened and get on with our lives," was simply not an option. These were wounds that needed to be cleansed; this was a gash that had to heal.

"Okay then," I said softly.

And I went back to bed.

But I needed to tell you this, to confess to having had that moment, that cowardly, selfish urge to leave everything the way it was. I had been tempted to abandon my biological child and to prevent the one I already loved from having the chance to love someone other than me.

And I needed to tell you because it is evidence of something very, very important to the course of this journey. . . .

It proves to you, and to me, that I am only human.

* * *

Two days later, we were driving back to the genetic counselor's office to meet our biological daughter.

Same diplomas, same DNA model. Very different set of circumstances.

We arrived before they did, so we stood around making awkward small talk with the counselor. Bay's big brown eyes seemed bigger than usual. I'm sure I was shaking in my Christian Louboutins. John was jumpy.

Because we now knew that our daughter had grown up a mere fifteen miles north of Mission Hills, in a neighborhood called East Riverside. This was not something John and I were particularly happy to learn. East Riverside is a high-crime, low-income neighborhood. Years ago, we had considered opening a car wash there, but John's financial advisors deemed it a bad risk to open a primarily cash business in an area known for, among other things, a fair amount of drug traffic.

East Riverside!

Were there sections of town as bad or worse? Sure.

Would I want my child growing up in any of them? Not a chance.

John's powerhouse attorney had dropped this bomb on us just the night before; he'd managed to drag the information out of one of the hospital lawyers and he immediately called us to report it. John, Toby, and I were in the kitchen, finishing dinner. Bay was in her art studio.

"Hello, John, Kathryn. . . ." His über-educated voice came booming through the phone's speaker. "Are you sitting down?"

(Now, I ask you, did any good conversation ever begin with that phrase?)

On his end of the line, I heard papers shuffling. I think I may have been wringing my hands, waiting for this legal equivalent to a superhero to speak again. When he did, I wished he hadn't.

East Riverside, he told us.

Single mother, he said. On the plus side, this single mother was an American citizen (not always a given for residents of that neighborhood), or at least he hadn't been told anything to the contrary.

"Anything else?" John asked, dragging a hand down his face.

No, that was all he had for us at the moment. Captain Adjudication apologized for not being able to do a full background check on the single mom from East Riverside, but when he'd prodded the hospital henchman for a name, the other lawyer suddenly remembered his ethics and shut up. But certainly, the three facts we did have did not bode well for the next day's meeting.

"Good work, Counselor," John said heavily. "Thanks."

When the super-lawyer signed off, I pictured him rushing to the nearest phone booth to change out of his cape and tights and back into his Hugo Boss pinstripe.

I pressed my fingertips to my temples and sighed. "Our little girl lives in East Riverside?"

"So what are we thinking?" Toby asked, taking his last bite of pecan-crusted tilapia. "Worst case scenario, she's a gang member?"

At that, I gasped. I think I turned completely white and my eyes flew open wide.

Toby gulped down his fish. "Mom, I was kidding!"

"Of course he was kidding." John quickly put his arms around me. "Sweetheart, she's a fifteen-year-old girl, not an ex-con."

"As far as we know . . ."

"You're being irrational."

"Well don't you think I'm entitled?" I lowered myself onto one of the bar stools, throwing up my hands. "Hell, I'd say I'm entitled to be stark raving mad! And so far I've managed to keep it down to a mild case of crazy. So how about giving me a little credit?"

Toby offered me a fist bump and said, "Respect."

I lowered one eyebrow at him. "Is that gang lingo?"

"No, it's Aretha Franklin."

Believe it or not, I laughed and clonked my knuckles against his.

I think this is a good place to make a point about humor: Never, ever underestimate its healing power. Because, looking back, I know in my heart that it was the laughter—when we could manage it—that got us through those six weeks. Bay's rapier wit, Toby's clever irreverence, John's goofy jokes, even my own occasional silliness—they were like an elixir that kept me from burying myself under the emotional weight of it all. We laughed to keep from crying, and that is the reason I never did cross the line from mildly crazy to full-on nuts.

Laughter. Enough said.

Now, less than twenty-four hours after our conversation with the Caped Litigator, we were preparing to see firsthand the effects of growing up in East Riverside.

When the office door opened, my heart leaped into my throat.

And then, it melted.

Melted, at the sight of the stunning, slender strawberry blonde who was smiling shyly at John and me. (No do-rag, no gang ink, thank heaven.) Just an utterly angelic-looking teenage girl.

Did I notice the woman who had come into the office with her? Not at all. Because for one split second it was as if this girl and Bay and I were the only three people on the entire planet. I felt a surge of pride at how beautiful both my daughters were.

If I had a billion pages to fill I could not adequately describe how I felt in those first few seconds; I think perhaps I was experiencing emotions that have yet to be named, feelings so rare and extraordinary that they simply cannot be defined.

Then the counselor who had started it all was saying, "Daphne, this is Bay. Bay, Daphne."

And Daphne, my daughter Daphne, who I'd held in my arms just once sixteen years ago, flashed a gorgeous smile and said, "It's nice to meet you."

I would like to say that my first thought was that my daughter was well mannered. But that was not the case. Because Daphne didn't just *say* it.

She signed it.

Which is why my first thought was not *She's polite.*

My first thought was *She's deaf.*

* * *

Amazingly, I was able to stay on my feet; miraculously I didn't weep, and this was because I had to think of Bay. I had to be strong and calm for Bay, who right that very second was going through something every bit as enormous as what I was going through. Equally enormous, but in reverse.

She was looking into the dark eyes and lovely face of the woman who had pushed *her* into the world and fed *her* from her own body. Her biological mother.

Something fiercely protective ignited in me. I was like a warrior, ready to attack if this woman did one thing to make Bay feel anything less than unconditionally adored.

But this woman, this Regina Vasquez, with the rich chestnut hair (like Bay's) and deep brown eyes (like Bay's), was looking at my daughter—her daughter—as though she were seeing a priceless work of art, a precious treasure.

Which, of course, she was.

And I understood that I wasn't the only one whose heart had just melted. Regina was taking Bay in, her eyes filled with tenderness and awe. She was making up for a decade and a half of not having this exquisite young woman in her life. She was trying to make sense of it, even as she knew that there was no way to make sense of it. And she was looking every bit as proud and delighted and terrified as I was.

The reality set in: This was Bay's mother.

Bay's mother? No. *I'm* Bay's mother.

And I'm Daphne's mother.

It didn't take a mind reader to know that this woman, this Regina Vasquez, was thinking the same thing. For one crazy second, I considered knocking her down, grabbing both girls, and running away with them, never to be found.

But that is not how a self-respecting Mission Hills mom conducts herself.

This is:

"Regina," I said in my most gracious voice, "we'd love to have you to our house for lunch."

❖ ❖ ❖

So we dined together.

I made some rookie errors with regard to Daphne's

deafness, and Regina reacted in a manner that, at the time, I thought was hostile. But I understand now. She had one agenda, and that was to protect Daphne from our ignorance. The only thing we were guilty of was having never known anyone who was deaf. We guessed, plain and simple, and we guessed wrong. I spoke too loud, I spoke too fast, I asked Regina if she was Mexican—wrong, wrong, and wrong (she's Puerto Rican, in fact). We found out that Daphne and Regina lived with Regina's mother, Adrianna, and that Daphne was a vegetarian (so much for the chicken enchiladas I had warming in the oven).

Through all of it, I sensed Regina's defensiveness (although at the time I might have said contempt). But now that I've had some time to consider it from her point of view, I know I can't blame her. First impressions are mostly about what you see on the surface (since there's really little else to go on), and Regina was walking into a pretty intimidating setting. I'm sure, at that point, she saw us primarily in terms of the neighborhood in which we lived. And weren't we seeing her in the same way? Not to mention that she was outnumbered. We had the "conventional family" thing going for us, and it must have seemed to her that we were flaunting it.

Of course, she had the significant advantage of speaking Bay's language, whereas every time Daphne tried to communicate with us in hers—those graceful but elusive signs and hand gestures—I held my breath hoping John wouldn't make some seemingly insensitive crack about the third base coach signaling him to steal second! He didn't, thank God, but if he had, he wouldn't have meant it as anything other than a joke to lighten an incredibly awkward mood.

We were all doing our best.

Isn't that what all parents do? Their best?

Of course it is. But sometimes, as we were soon to find out, even your best gets tested.

* * *

Bay tested us, a week later, by getting arrested. I'm sure that wasn't her plan when she tried to buy beer with a fake ID, but that's what happened. And since she now found herself the daughter of two mothers, she opted to use her proverbial single phone call to reach out to the one she thought would go easier on her: Regina.

When John and I went to pick Bay up at the police precinct (a phrase, believe me, I never thought I'd have occasion to use), I will admit that I behaved badly.

How badly? Well, let's see . . . basically, I accused Regina of being responsible for the meningitis that caused Daphne to go deaf (and blamed that negligence on her having been a raging drunk) and then I threatened to sue her for custody of both Bay and Daphne. But the irony was that while I was shouting at Regina and calling *her* a bad parent, Bay, the daughter *I* had raised, slipped out of the police station right under my nose.

She was gone for most of the night. We didn't know where she was, and I was terrified as we searched for her. (I wondered: Was this to become some kind of sick pattern in my life? Looking for my daughters and not knowing what I'd find?)

Bay went missing for hours. It was a miserable night. But miraculously, something wonderful came out of it.

* * *

The next night, as we were getting ready for bed, I said to John, "Bay had a thought. . . ."

"Did she?" He flung aside a throw pillow. "Did it have anything to do with never getting arrested again as long as she lives?"

"It had to do with the guesthouse," I said, as he pulled down the quilt and climbed into bed.

"Ah, so she wants to move out now?"

"Actually, she wants Daphne and Regina to move in."

He froze, clutching the hand-embroidered edge of the bedsheet. "She wants them to move in?" he echoed. "To the guesthouse? *Our* guesthouse?"

"Yes. I just don't know how I feel about it."

Above our expansive garage was a finished apartment, a three-bedroom, two-bath living space that took a beating every five years when John hosted a reunion of his college baseball buddies; other than that, the place rarely saw any action. I pictured the guest suite now, with its spacious rooms and charming eaves, and knew that Bay's idea had much to recommend it. It would mean that Daphne would be with us, safe, a mere twenty feet away on the opposite side of the driveway. Inviting the Vasquezes to live in the guesthouse would allow me to have daily contact with Daphne. Of course it also meant that Regina would have equally convenient access to Bay.

And I just wasn't sure I was ready for that.

John, however, seemed totally on board. "It's not a bad

idea," he said reasonably. "It's just sitting there, empty. Well, except for the squirrel overflow."

I rolled my eyes at his reference to my beloved collection of anything squirrel-related—knickknacks, cookie jars, bookends . . .

"I don't know. . . ." I leaned back against the pillows and tried to imagine it. "I mean, it sure sounds great on paper, but how would it work in practice?"

"Well, let's see." John pretended to puzzle it out. "You can parent the girls on Mondays, Wednesdays, and Fridays. Regina can parent them on Tuesdays, Thursdays, and Saturdays."

"Right. And on Sunday, we can all go straight to psychotherapy!" I laughed. "I bet we could get a group rate."

He reached up to turn off the bedside lamp; the room became silvery with the moonlight that spilled in through the windows. I thought about Daphne in East Riverside; the same moon was shining in her window. A window which, according to John, had bars on it.

There were no bars on the guesthouse windows, although after the previous night, I was seriously considering putting some on the ones in Bay's room.

"So what would this experiment in coparenting be like?" I heard myself asking. "Will I have to consult Regina on every decision I make regarding Bay? Will she have to powwow with me anytime there's an issue with Daphne?"

In that regard, I wondered if I'd even be qualified to weigh in. I suspected a lot of Daphne's freedoms and restrictions were directly related to her deafness. And as I'd proved in such a grand and humiliating fashion at last week's luncheon, I simply was not educated. I made a mental note to go online first thing in the morning to research everything I could find about raising a deaf child.

"Maybe it doesn't have to be about coparenting at all," John suggested. "It can just be a way for us all to get to know each other. For us to get to know Daphne and for Regina to get to know Bay."

"I want that," I whispered, and my voice sounded wistful in the pale-lit room. "And I hate the idea of Daphne spending one more minute in East Riverside."

John reached over and stroked my hair. "It's a rough neighborhood," he agreed. "They've been lucky so far, but . . ."

But luck runs out. And what would happen when it did? A carjacking? A mugging? A home invasion? Three females— one of whom was a woman in her seventies and another of whom wouldn't hear the door being broken down or a window getting smashed in—would surely constitute an easy target. I shuddered to think how truly vulnerable they were.

Through the window I could see the slate shingles of the guesthouse roof. "Right next door, huh?"

"Neighbors." John propped himself on his elbow and smiled at me. "You and Regina can be just like Lucy and Ethel. Or Wilma and Betty. It'll be fun. You can borrow cups of sugar from each other and come up with all kinds of crazy schemes."

"You mean crazier than the scheme to share a driveway with the woman who is the biological mother of our daughter?" I closed my eyes. "This whole situation is so . . . unprecedented. I'm terrified that I'll say the wrong thing, or make the wrong gesture, or the wrong meal." I thumped the heel of my hand against my forehead and groaned, remembering how utterly incompetent I'd felt during that lunch. "Chicken enchiladas! Why did I have to make chicken?"

"Because you didn't know Daphne was a vegetarian, that's why." John laid his hand gently on my belly, like he used to do when I was pregnant, and I reveled in the warmth, the comfort of it. "That's kind of the whole point. There's going to be one hell of a learning curve, and I think the best way to get ahead of it is to have Daphne and Regina move in here."

"The old 'keep your friends close and your long-lost daughter and the woman who raised her closer' trick, huh?"

"Is that what we're calling her, then?" I felt him smile in the shadowy room. "Our 'long- lost' daughter?"

"Hmm." I wrinkled my nose. "Too soap opera-y?"

"Little bit." John chuckled. Then he kissed me on the tip of my nose. "We can do this, Kathryn. We have to do this. And besides, it could have been worse. A lot worse. Regina might seem a little abrasive right now, but I think that's just because she doesn't know how to handle this any better than we do."

It was an indication of how loyal he was that he called *her* abrasive but made no mention of *me* threatening her with litigation and calling her a drunk.

I let out a long sigh. "I'll call her tomorrow and extend the offer to move in to the guesthouse."

"Thatta girl, Lucy."

"Very funny. Now go to sleep, wise guy, before I play a rousing rendition of 'Babaloo' on your skull!" I rolled over and kissed his cheek.

He kissed me back. "Well, then you'd really have some 'splainin' to do, wouldn't you?"

Despite my exhaustion, I felt my mind shifting into "organize" mode.

"We're all going to learn sign language," I announced. "I'll buy a book tomorrow. Or maybe a DVD. I'm sure they have a DVD."

"I'm sure they do."

"And I noticed that Daphne wears hearing aids. I think they take special batteries, don't they? I'm going to get some, just so we'll always have them handy, in case—"

"Good night, Kathryn."

"Good night."

I snuggled under the blanket and drifted off to sleep.

Chapter Four

To give you an idea of how nerve-wracking it was to know that my newly extended family (which was the description I'd settled on since I couldn't come up with a better one) was moving in across the driveway, I will tell you about a shopping trip I made.

When the Vasquezes accepted our invitation to come live in Mission Hills, I promptly went up to the guesthouse and cleaned it within an inch of its life. I swept, I dusted, I waxed, I vacuumed. But John's college buddies had been merciless on the linens, and I knew there was not enough Clorox in the world to make those sheets and towels look new again.

So I went shopping.

Now, I will cop to having a tendency to "over-engineer" certain projects. When Bay was nine and went to sleepaway summer camp, for example, I packed exactly sixteen outfits (one for every day of the two-week stay and two additional in case she got muddy or a juice box exploded on her). The outfits included socks and underwear and were tucked into sixteen individual ziplock plastic bags. Each bag was labeled to indicate which outfit was to be worn on what day and for which activity. The jean shorts and Spice Girls T-shirt were for Tuesday's arts and crafts class; the madras Bermudas and green polo shirt were for Thursday's archery competition. Swimsuits were for swimming, of course (one-piece for the lake, two-piece for the pool) . . . You get the picture.

Well, I got a picture, too. It was included with Bay's first letter home, and she was smiling triumphantly, decked out in the tank top and white skirt I'd earmarked especially for tennis lessons. But she wasn't wearing the skirt ensemble for tennis, she was wearing it for the all-camp canoe regatta. And the socks she had on didn't even belong to her.

Message received, Bay, loud and clear.

My shopping trip to purchase new linens for the guesthouse was an exercise in that same kind of overthinking.

Every towel and sheet set I owned had been purchased at a store called Scandia Down in Kansas City, and I would be lying if I said they hadn't all been exorbitantly expensive. But sleeping on those sheets was like sleeping on a cloud, and the towels were plump and thirsty enough to soak up a large pond. I wanted only the best for Daphne, so, being as I was in need of new linens, out of habit I headed straight to that upscale bedding shop.

Then I thought, *Maybe Regina will think I'm showing off by making up her bed with four-hundred-dollar sheets. Will it be thoughtless of me to stock the bathroom with towels that cost more money than she earns in a month?*

So I pulled out of Country Club Plaza and drove to Walmart, where I sat in the parking lot, hating myself for a good twenty minutes. What kind of message would these linens send?

I didn't want to insult anyone, I didn't want to impress anyone. I just wanted to be welcoming. But I was driving myself crazy over pillowcases!

In the end, I split the difference and purchased new towels and three sets of sheets at Bed Bath & Beyond, reasoning that with regard to price and quality, the chain fell somewhere in the middle between my first two attempts. I was able to relax at last, knowing that nothing could be read into a receipt from Bed Bath & Beyond.

* * *

A week later, the moving van arrived, and my heart soared to know that at long last I had all three of my children, if not under the same contiguous roof, at least residing at the same address.

Several of my squirrel collectibles bit the dust in favor of Regina's funky, brightly colored original artwork. I will confess to feeling a jealousy more intense than I'd ever known when Bay made this connection. Her artistic talent, the origins of which had been so mystifying and untraceable until now, had been a gift from her biological mother all along. That piece of herself that Bay loved most, that defined her, was a piece passed down to her from Regina.

And what had *I* passed down to Bay? The lyrics to The Bangles' "Walk Like an Egyptian" (which oddly enough was the only song that could ever lull her to sleep, and which, therefore, I sang to her nightly until she was six; to this day she still sings along when it comes on the radio)? A working knowledge of finger bowls and shrimp forks even Martha Stewart would envy? Oh and, once, a tennis racquet.

John told me I shouldn't feel that way. He said I'd *absolutely* given of myself to Bay, if not in nature, then definitely in nurture. Any traits and talents that had come to her innately from Regina as seedlings had been coaxed into full blossom by me, cultivated and fostered (I'd bristled at his use of that word, and he immediately took it back). I was the one who taught her to be confident. She learned by my example to expect only good things from herself and to share her spark with the world.

"The apple doesn't fall far from the tree," John had said. Of course, in our case the apple had been picked from the branch and thrown clear across the orchard.

But as I'd learned way back when in chem lab: equal and opposite. The good news was that I was seeing things in Daphne that reminded me so much of myself at that age that it was like stepping through the looking glass and into my own past.

It wasn't just her looks, and there's no denying that the resemblance to sixteen-year-old me was startling. But it was much more than how she looked. She moved like I did. She loved to cook and she had an almost obsessive love of avocados. She was a lemons-out-of-lemonade kind of gal, just like I was. Daphne was naturally inclined to look for the bright side of a situation and wring every drop of positivity out of it. There was an innocence about her that I was sure would never go away, and she possessed a desire to please others not because she was subservient, but simply because it made her happy to see them happy.

And although, as a teenager, I had never faced a struggle that matched the magnitude of Daphne's hearing loss, I believe in my heart that the lion's share of her courage and tenacity had come to her directly from me. Grudgingly, I made myself admit that Regina had taken the nurturing ball and run with it on this one. I knew she'd done her homework, I knew she'd become an expert on everything pertaining to deafness, and I knew that she worked every day of her life to insure that Daphne, my Daphne, our Daphne would never feel diminished by it.

I will never, as long as I live, be able to repay her for that.

But I will tell you that this adjusted living situation was not without its complications. This mother and child reunion brought with it more than just the opportunity for me to revel in how much Daphne was like me.

If I'd thought John's college buddies were rough on the place, they were nothing compared to Regina. On the first morning of our new living arrangement I walked in to find her actually stripping the wallpaper of the walls! The wallpaper that had taken me three decorators and I don't know how many swatches to select. It matched the window valances (although a quick glance told me those were gone, too) and the throw pillows (still tossed artfully into the corners of the couch, but I doubted they were long for this world).

I did what I'd come to do—which was invite this one-woman wrecking crew to join us for dinner on the patio that evening—and sought out my husband.

He knew immediately that I was upset. No, not upset, angry bordering on furious.

"What's wrong?"

"She's ripping that place apart," I reported. "I mean literally—tearing it down."

"We agreed she could do whatever she wanted," he reminded me. "That was the deal. . . . Don't tell me you're having second thoughts."

Of course I was having second thoughts. She was messing with my wallpaper. It was practically a declaration of war!

"We asked this woman we barely know to move in," I recapped unnecessarily. "Maybe we should have tried some other way to get to know each other before sharing patio furniture." Sharing daughters was more than enough, I was realizing now.

John maintained his calm and looked at me evenly. "What do you want to do now—undo it? Honey, this is our life now. Wallpaper's just the beginning."

The scream I never screamed the night I'd awoken in a panic and offered Bay an exit clause was coming up again, beginning in the pit of my belly and begging to be released. But this time John's words were the ones that threatened to break the sound barrier: *Undo it.*

Could I?

Could I send Regina packing just like that? Could I put in an emergency call to the wallpaper guys, begging them to speed over here and repair the destruction my boarder of less than a day had inflicted? Could I send that one-woman wrecking crew back to East Riverside?

Not if I wanted to keep Daphne here I couldn't.

And so began the clash of the parenting styles. It was more of a cold war than an actual invasion, but make no mistake, the battle lines were drawn. Parenting is something that people hold very dear, something on which they pride themselves. It is intensely personal. "I'm forming my kid, here, so just step off, pal, and don't you dare comment or judge or suggest." Backseat drivers, armchair quarterbacks—they're nothing compared to the "across-the-driveway coparent." What Regina and I have since discovered, though, is that there are certain universal truths to being a parent. No matter what your methods (or what books you've read on the subject), there are fundamental truths that cross all the parenting lines—the ethnic, the regional, the socioeconomic:

A parent loves, panics, protects, screws up, bribes, begs, screams, and kisses the boo-boos. Parenting is a privilege. It is a quest, a challenge. It is a lifetime of agreeing to disagree and of gritting your teeth and compromising.

Especially, we found out, when it comes to motorcycles.

* * *

You can't talk about yourself as a parent unless you back-pedal a little to consider how you yourself were parented.

My mother married a man "with potential," and for many years, my father made a very comfortable living. I benefitted from his work ethic in the form of horseback riding lessons and a private tennis coach. Life, for the most part, was good.

During my junior year in high school, my father declared bankruptcy. This was a horrible blow. This terrible (and humiliating, to hear my mother tell it) reversal of fortune was the result of my father employing extremely poor judgment when it came to investing other people's money. I never got the specifics, and frankly, I prefer it that way. At the time I wouldn't have understood, and now, as an adult, I realize the specifics are not important. He was careless, and it cost him more than his business; it cost us our family.

This isn't exactly classified information, but needless to say, it isn't the kind of story one tends to trot out at dinner parties. "Leave it alone," John likes to say, "it's all in the past," but as I am learning, as we are all learning, the past has a way of catching up with you. And by "catching up" I mean hunting you down and pouncing on you when you least expect it. Always, the past is just a step, or a page, or a blood test behind you. You need not fear it, but you must always bear in mind that the past is never quite as finished with you as you think you are with it.

The thing is, there are events in our lives that impact us, and the bankruptcy issue and the divorce that followed it are two things that impacted me greatly.

When my parents divorced, I found myself bouncing back and forth between them, not only on alternate weekends, but in terms of sympathy. I would feel nothing but heartache for my mother when I'd find her sitting alone in the big master bedroom, crying into my father's empty dresser drawers. And I would feel thoroughly awful for my poor, lonely father when I would visit him and find him eating cold beans out of a can (because his was part of a generation of men who had never been taught to cook). The thing I will never forgive either of them for is that they ignored my own sadness and used me as artillery against each other. They were more concerned with "winning" than with how their behavior made me feel.

Their hostility came to a head when it was time for me to attend the senior prom. I expected to go with the boy I'd been "keeping company with" (which is what my mother called it, as though her daughter was Scarlett O'Hara and not Katie Tamblyn). The boy's name was Trevor Anderson. He had lent me his varsity jacket one crisp, autumn day and then never asked for it back, which officially made us a couple. But when spring came, Trevor broke my heart by asking Linda DeCapella to the prom instead of me. Well, Linda DeCapella put out; I didn't.

My mother was as crestfallen as I was, possibly more. Trevor was husband material in her opinion (she pointed this out even though I was only a high school senior), and I should have found a way to keep my hooks in him without stooping to Ms. DeCapella's level.

I wish that just once she'd indicated to me that she saw Trevor's breaking up with me as his loss, not mine.

My father did. "It's his loss, Katie," he said when I told him the whole horrible story during my court-sanctioned visit that weekend. "That boy will be kicking himself one day, you mark my words."

It's his loss, Katie. To this day, I remember that as one of the sweetest things my father ever said to me.

My mother dealt with the situation not by attempting to comfort me but by flipping through my school yearbook, in search of an acceptable replacement prom date for me. Do you think I'm exaggerating? I'm not. Her rationale was that I was going to have to work quickly if I had any hopes of securing a boy from one of the "better" families. She'd narrowed it down to Jimmy Hartley, from up the street (she knew his mother from bridge club), and Robert M. Dennison III, our class treasurer who was a legacy at Purdue.

I casually suggested that I might like to go to prom with a boy from my European history class, Javier Menendez, who had moved to town recently from the Bronx, New York. As you might imagine, my mother did not see Javier as a viable option, and she told me so.

She also told me that I could forget about my father coming to the house on prom night to see me in my dress and pose for photos with me in front of the fireplace.

"He's not welcome here," she said, turning another page in the yearbook in case she'd missed anyone who might prove to be more suitable than Robbie or Jim.

"That's not fair," I told her. "You divorced him. I didn't."

But I knew it had nothing to do with fairness. My mother was in the enviable position of having me on her home turf, and forbidding my father to come see me all dressed up and beaming beside my handsome date (whoever he turned out to be) was the checkmate move she'd been waiting for. Prom happened once in a lifetime and she was going to deprive him of being a part of it, just because she could.

How I felt about it, apparently, didn't matter. I would have expressed my feelings, but that was not something my mother encouraged.

In the end I went to the dance with Robbie Dennison and (Bay will no doubt roll her eyes here, but I think Daphne will find it sweet) I was elected prom queen in a landslide victory. Take that, Trevor Anderson!

The point is that my mother had very definite ideas about things, and they were rarely open to negotiation. I'm that way when it comes to things like running with scissors and ingesting poison (and, let us not forget, riding on motorcycles), but I am a firm believer in giving a child the freedom to express herself.

Maybe I wouldn't be, if I hadn't had one kid who was a musical prodigy and another who was a gifted artist. Maybe I came to believe in self-expression because I found myself raising children who needed me to believe in it. And because I loved them and wanted them to be happy and fulfilled, I found a way to become the mother that fit them best, the mother I am today.

So perhaps you don't just learn how to parent from your parents. Perhaps, some of it you learn from your kids—but only if you're paying attention, and only if you're willing to be taught. Maybe, all the time we think we are guiding and molding our children, the reality is that they are guiding and molding us.

That never occurred to me until this very moment.

And here I find myself once again reminded that motherhood, in the very best of ways, will always find a way to surprise me.

* * *

Here's what happened with the motorcycle: Prior to Daphne, Regina, and Adrianna moving in, John and I had taken Daphne for a tour of the prep school Bay and Toby attend. Our hope was that she would decide to transfer from her high school, Carlton School for the Deaf, and allow us to pay her tuition at Buckner Hall.

I can say now that this was not our most shining moment. We hadn't thought it through clearly enough, being as we were so anxious to make up for lost time with Daphne. We meant well, but you know where the road to good intentions can lead. Carlton was and remains the absolute, uncontested right place for Daphne to be. But we live and we learn. Of all the platitudes and axioms and old sayings that have been articulated throughout this experience, I can tell you that this one rings truest.

Nevertheless, we called the appropriate administrators and set up a tour of Buckner. On the way home a motorcycle pulled up beside us, and to my horror, Daphne was riding on the back of it.

My heart thudded in my chest out of pure fear for her safety, and I actually called out to her through the window. But of course she didn't hear me. Neither did the driver,

Emmett, who was also deaf. I immediately had a sense that this young man, wearing his leather jacket and gripping the handlebars with such intensity, was filled with a combination of teen angst and passion, like a deaf James Dean. And, of course, therein lay the root of my terror.

But Regina, we discovered, had signed off on Daphne riding with this kid. Frankly, I couldn't believe it, and I told her so, and of course, she defended her decision.

She countered by questioning the wisdom of buying Toby a thirty-thousand-dollar sports car.

It was a standoff, a battle of wills.

Ultimately, Regina came around. She didn't allow us to forbid Daphne from riding with her friend, but she did admit to John that she had adamantly resisted the motorcycle for months before she finally broke down and consented. She told him she trusted Emmett implicitly, and that he had a stellar driving record. Of course that hadn't stopped her from following them at a distance the first few weeks after she gave Daphne permission to ride.

"You know what's funny?" she said to John then. "For years, I've wished there was someone else around to bounce this stuff off of."

I think I know what she was getting at it. Bouncing something off of someone is different than actually giving up your voice. It's a good thing when someone says, "Keep it up, you're doing great," but quite another when the response is "Let's try it my way."

We both wanted a voice. And we would both have one. The difficult thing was going to be learning to harmonize.

CHAPTER FIVE

How Tandoori Chicken Can Change Your Life

I know there is no way I will escape this memoir without at least touching on that abstract concept known as Fate. Whether you call it karma, kismet, fortune, destiny, serendipity, good old-fashioned dumb luck, or all of the above, surely you must be wondering where, in light of my circumstance, I stand on this issue. As I am not a philosopher or a Zen master or a theologian, I will have to explain it to you in the rudimentary terms by which I myself have come to understand it. If it seems oversimplified, that's because it is.

Six days prior to the due date of my second child, I found myself craving Indian food in the absolute worst way. Visions of Vindaloo danced in my head as I called John at work and instructed him to bring home as much curry-flavored take-out food as he could fit in the cargo hold of the Range Rover he was driving at the time.

"Isn't Indian food a little spicy?" he asked cautiously. (I'd entered that phase of my pregnancy when even the slightest hint of provocation could send me into a hormone-driven meltdown.)

"It's very spicy, actually."

"Well, you're due in six days."

"What's your point?"

Needless to say, John picked up the Indian food and I

devoured every last morsel like the extremely pregnant woman I was.

Which was why I developed one hell of a case of heartburn.

Which was why I couldn't fall asleep.

Which was why, at two o'clock in the morning, I decided the upper shelf of the walk-in cedar closet needed to be completely reorganized, and since in a mere six days I would be the mother of two (count 'em, *two*!) children under the age of twenty-four months, I'd better get a move on and do it now while I had the chance.

Which was why I was stupidly attempting to lift a thirty-gallon plastic storage bin filled with woolen blankets and flannel sheets in the middle of the night.

Which was why I went into labor six days earlier than I was scheduled to and wound up giving birth to my daughter on a day when the nurses in the maternity ward were being forced to work quadruple shifts.

Which is why in a state of utter exhaustion, one of them unintentionally gave me the wrong child.

Call it fate. Call it chance. Call it whatever you want. But that's how it happened. Life is just one big cosmic flowchart. I can't explain it any better than that. And I'm sure Regina can give me a similar breakdown of the events leading to the illness that resulted in Daphne losing her ability to hear. But what it all boils down to is this—whether you kill a ladybug in Tokyo and it causes a bridge to collapse in Belgium, or you crave Indian food in Mission Hills and it results in a hospital staffer putting the wrong ID anklet on your newborn baby, there are forces at work in the universe over which we mere mortals have no control. If I had been craving oatmeal, or mashed potatoes, then maybe none of this would have ever happened.

Or, then again, maybe it would have. I don't presume to know, and frankly, it's too exhausting to even try and guess.

I heard an expression once: *Want to make God laugh? Tell him your plans.*

In other words, the best and only thing we can do is simply enjoy the Tandoori and hope the dominoes fall in our favor.

* * *

I met John Kennish in the fall of 1990.

I graduated from Wofford College in South Carolina the spring before and was living at home with my mother and her second husband, Dr. Gregory Dixon, a very successful orthopedic surgeon. Most of my girlfriends were away in graduate school or paying their entry-level dues in the corporate world.

I had been working part time at The Gap, mostly to keep busy while trying to determine what I really wanted to do with my life. My mother was distraught that I wasn't "serious" with anyone (I was twenty-one and, according to her, "not getting any younger"), so she saw to it that I maintained an active social life by setting me up on a series of dreadful blind dates with the sons or nephews or distant cousins of her bridge partners, country club friends, and so on. After one particularly horrific date with the godson of a church acquaintance, I caved in and called Trevor Anderson. Ol' Trev was also living at home with his folks, studying for the LSATs. By now, I'd forgiven him for the Linda DeCapella debacle and I figured it would be far less miserable catching the occasional dinner or movie with Trevor than suffering through any more blind dates arranged by my mother.

Then one day, Gregory's receptionist was rushed to the ER with a burst appendix and my stepfather asked me if I would mind filling in for her behind the front desk. My mother remarked that I shouldn't have any trouble taking time away from my "retail career" since she was sure there were plenty of sixteen-year-old Gap employees without college educations who would be willing to cover my shifts.

Dr. Greg's practice was a thriving one, and so my first day there was busy. The waiting room was packed with elderly women awaiting consultations for hip replacement surgery, and little kids and teenagers with various broken bones and other orthopedic complaints.

Toward the end of the day a man in his mid-twenties walked in. Actually, he sauntered in. He had a confidence about him that bordered on cockiness, which I figured stemmed from the fact that he was (as we said back in the nineties) a total babe.

The next thing I knew every kid in the office had rushed to this handsome newcomer. Kids hobbled over on crutches, just to get a closer look. He was signing casts and shaking hands, and every so often he'd look up from the mob, catch my eye, and smile.

I smiled back, but for the life of me I had no idea why people would be flocking to this man and asking for his autograph. I squinted at him, trying to place his face. Was he that guy from the TV show *L.A. Law*? No. The meteorologist from Channel 9? I didn't think so.

When the commotion subsided, the total babe approached my desk. My heart actually fluttered.

"Hi, I'm here to see Dr. Dixon. He's expecting me." He smiled warmly, expectantly, and I had the feeling he was waiting for me to ask him for an autograph.

So I did. I slid a prescription pad across the desk, and he signed his name with a flourish: *John Kennish.*

Still couldn't place him.

Furthermore, his name was not on the appointment list. But when I buzzed Dr. Greg, he told me to send this Kennish fellow right back to his private office.

When his unscheduled visit was finished, John Kennish (who I now thought might be a member of one those new grunge rock bands out of Seattle) stopped at my desk.

"I hope this doesn't sound forward," he said, smooth as silk, "but would you like to have dinner with me tonight? It'll have to be a late one. I'm working."

Naturally, I was flattered, and I felt my cheeks turn red. "I'd love to," I said truthfully, "but I can't. I have plans." Which I did. I'd agreed just that morning to join Trevor for one of our friendly default get-togethers. (Although they were becoming more frequent, and on the last one Trevor had actually kissed me good night. But the last thing I wanted to think about while looking into this John Kennish's big brown eyes was kissing Trevor Anderson.)

"Big date?" John asked, flirting shamelessly.

"No, not at all!" I answered, too quickly. "I'm just going out with an old friend. He's taking me to the Royals game."

At this, John burst out laughing, although I couldn't begin to imagine why. I did know I liked the sound of it.

"Good seats?" he asked when he finally quit cracking up.

"Right behind third base, I think. So I guess they're pretty good. My friend won them. The tickets, I mean. He was caller number fifteen in a radio call-in contest and . . ." I was rambling, which indicated to me just how attracted I was to this guy.

"Well, your friend is a lucky guy," John informed me, then grinned. "You enjoy the game, beautiful."

I think I actually giggled. And then he left.

Do I have to tell you that halfway through the first inning, the third baseman turned around and scanned the bleachers until he found me, and when our eyes met, he tipped his hat and winked?

And is it necessary for me to report that after the game I politely told Trevor to go on home without me and I waited for John (feeling deliciously reckless and a little bit naughty) like some kind of groupie outside the clubhouse door?

And you probably wouldn't be at all surprised to learn that *he* wasn't at all surprised to find me waiting there, and that we went out for drinks and halfway through my third glass of Chardonnay I knew I no longer needed to bide my time at The Gap, because I now knew exactly what I wanted to do with my life. In a matter of a few short hours I had fallen completely and totally in love with John Kennish. Trevor was genuinely disappointed when I broke the news that our quasi-courtship was over. He told me that, matrimonially speaking, a professional athlete was a bad bet, and my mother agreed.

But I didn't care what they thought. I was meant to meet John Kennish. I'm certain of it. So many forces combined to see to it, that I can only assume the universe deemed it necessary. And if I believe that, then I must also believe that I was meant to give birth to one baby and bring home another.

Because despite the confusion, and the disruption and the general weirdness of it all, I know I wouldn't trade one minute of the time I've had with Bay and Daphne, or the times still yet to come.

It's pointless to second-guess the universe.

CHAPTER SIX

Fatherhood: Easy enough to achieve, difficult to perfect.

John, though, took to it like a duck to water (or like a big-league third baseman to the car wash business). Which is to say, naturally. To be perfectly honest, I was a little surprised at first. I always knew he'd be a *good* father, I just never dreamed that he would love it—*love it*—as much as he did. He was a man's man, after all, a "big ol' lug" as they might say in an old movie. He was a jock, for God's sake!

But when Toby came into the world, my big ol' lug morphed into a big ol' creampuff. He sang lullabies, he changed diapers, he cradled our infant son in the crook of his throwing arm and read to him from *Peter Rabbit* and *The Little Prince* and *Sports Illustrated*.

Ladies, is there anything sexier than a man holding a baby? I think not.

So Toby pretty much ran the place. Like most first-time parents, we were willing slaves to that powdery little bundle of baby-boy-ness. He set the pace, made the rules, lorded over us with a drooly, toothless grin, and John and I couldn't have been happier to do his bidding.

When John traveled with the team, he made me promise to sit his son in front of the television and let him watch the games. It was silly, I knew, but I did it. I loved watching my husband play ball, and as I fed Toby his organic strained carrots, I'd provide color commentary, a running play-by-play of the game:

"Daddy just tagged that bad man who was trying to steal third base," I'd report proudly, and Toby would gurgle with joy.

"And what do we think of those icky old New York Yankees?" I'd prompt, and Toby would respond with a loud, wet raspberry, spewing orange mush all over the place.

When Toby turned four, John Kennish was the first father in line for Tee Ball sign-ups. In suburban communities like ours Tee Ball is a preschool rite of passage. Toby, in all modesty, was a natural. His swing was level and packed a fair amount of power for such a little tyke. On Saturdays when John wasn't playing out of town, he'd take Toby outside to "have a catch," and by third grade my son was shagging flies and fielding grounders like a champ. Rumor had it the local Little League coaches were all vying to have Toby on their team roster.

And that's when things started to go south.

Because as good as he was, Toby just didn't love it. He liked the father-son time, and he loved making John and me proud on game day. The problem was that given the choice Toby would much rather be sitting at the baby grand piano in our living room than in the garage oiling his mitt. Music came as easily to him as baseball did. He could play by ear, and when he started guitar lessons his teachers were blown away by the speed with which he picked it up.

If John was disappointed by this turn of extracurricular events, he did everything he could not to show it. I knew he missed those weekend afternoons coaching Toby in the yard;

I'd often see him throw a yearning glance out the window toward the corner of the yard where they used to hold batting practice, but I think he knew there was no point in pushing it.

Sports are optional; love is unconditional.

And then Daphne arrived and she had "Varsity" written all over her. I was so happy for John. Watching him play that first game of HORSE with Daphne in the driveway was a moment that was filled with tenderness. She not only had his physical grace and keen eye, she had his competitive spirit as well. It was as though he were at last being validated, as though everything he knew about himself was being reflected back to him in the best possible way. I would stand at the kitchen sink, sudsing a roasting pan, and I'd hear the thump of the basketball against the pavement and the squealing of sneaker soles as one them broke for the basket.

It was one of the most rewarding sounds I'd ever heard.

But if there was a negative aspect to John and Daphne bonding over "hoops," it was watching Bay adjust to it.

It's no secret that Bay was not a jock. Even at a young age she was bright and creative; she was not weird, she was unconventional. But according to John (and rightfully so), even unconventional kids require exercise.

I couldn't argue with that, and besides that, I loved sports. I had been captain of the Wofford College women's tennis team and still enjoyed the occasional mixed doubles game at the country club. I saw nothing but good things coming from Bay taking part in some manner of organized sports. So Bay was herded off to youth soccer.

It was an unqualified disaster.

I watched from the bleachers as my poor little girl got trounced by a swarm of other little girls in ponytails and matching jerseys.

When soccer was over, Bay climbed into the SUV looking not humiliated (as I had dreaded she would) but utterly bewildered and more than a little bit pissed off.

"Why did you make me do that?" she demanded.

"Don't worry, kiddo," John said in that confident "I can fix this" tone of his. "We'll work on it as soon as we get home."

"I'd rather just paint," Bay informed him. (She'd picked up her first brush the year before, when she was five, and had fallen in love with the activity of painting.)

But there would be no painting that day. There would be dribbling drills and stop-and-kick drills and a crash course in the proper running technique. I stood there watching her struggle—and watching *him* struggle to teach her how *not* to struggle—for what seemed like forever.

By dinnertime, Bay had had it.

And John knew it.

"I'm sorry I'm so bad at this," she grumbled. "I get it if you don't like me anymore."

Half an hour later, John summoned us to the garage, where he had an enormous canvas propped against the wall, a six-by-six-foot square of snowy white unconditional love. He'd already opened several large paint cans. Then he handed Bay the hated soccer ball. It took her a minute to grasp his purpose, but when she did, her chubby little face (still smeared with dirt from the day's athletic exertions) lit up with a huge grin.

John and I watched as she dipped the ball carefully into

the yellow paint. Then she hurled it as hard as she could at the blank canvas. It wasn't a graceful throw but it did hit its mark, leaving a soccer ball–textured yellow splotch on the white field. The wet paint began to drip in uneven trickles.

"Now, that's what I call dribbling," John joked.

Then John grabbed a tennis ball, dipped it into the red paint, and followed suit.

Then Bay created some amazing designs by shaking purple paint off the netted head of a lacrosse stick. I drop-kicked a pink-dipped football and nearly broke the garage window, but all in all it was the best art lesson I'd ever witnessed.

Bay gained the knowledge that no matter what she chose to do, her father would find a way to support her in it.

And then came Danny McMullen.

Because even quirky, enigmatic little girls fall in love, and Danny McMullen was Bay's first crush. This was in second grade. She came home after the first day of school and announced to us that Danny McMullen had blue eyes and a Pokémon backpack, and she was going to marry him.

Toby immediately launched into a chorus of *"Bay and Danny sittin' in a tree."* I smiled and told her I thought it was a lovely idea and floated the idea of a wedding gown with a sleek silhouette and understated beading.

But John said nothing, nothing at all. That was how I knew that in his mind this Danny McMullen character had just become Public Enemy Number One.

As you know, second-grade romance has a very short shelf life. Two days later, Bay came home in tears, heartbroken because Danny McMullen had told Ethan Feldman to tell Emily Pendleton to tell Bay Kennish that he didn't like her anymore; his feelings had shifted, and the new object of his affection was Brianna Winslow, a third-grader.

John took the news badly. Worse than Bay in fact. After a triple scoop of Chunky Monkey, Bay was over it. But John . . . not so much.

"He dumped her for a third-grader? What is this Brianna, some kind of an elementary school cougar?"

"A cougar cub," I quipped.

But John wasn't having it. "Doesn't this McMullen punk know how lucky he is that Bay even looked in his direction in the first place?"

"You do realize we're talking about a love affair that lasted less than forty-eight hours, right? Oh, and, by the way, she's eight."

"That's not the point. He made her cry, Kathryn." John's expression was one of sheer helplessness. "This was her first heartbreak."

"I know," I told him gently. "And unfortunately, it won't be her last."

This, of course, was the problem. John knew it was only the beginning. The world was full of Danny McMullens and Brianna Winslows. There were boys who would promise to call and then wouldn't; there were dances she wouldn't be invited to and valentines she wouldn't receive; parties she'd find out about the day after they occurred and all kinds of middle school and high school drama waiting in the years ahead.

Kids can be cruel. It happens to everyone.

The trouble was that John just couldn't bear the thought of it happening to Bay.

That night, when we tucked our daughter into bed,

John kissed her on the forehead. "Forget about Danny Mc-Mullen," he whispered in her ear. "It's his loss."

The following week Bay came home giddy about a new love in her life. His name was Alexander, and he'd spent the last three recess periods in the principal's office. Luckily, John was playing in Chicago that week, so he wasn't around to hear that his little girl had officially entered her inevitable "bad boy" phase.

But he was there for the next one, and the one after that. Some of them he liked, some of them were lucky to get out of our house alive; some of them broke her heart, and some, it has to be said, had their hearts broken by her.

John was careful to teach her that there was a right way and a wrong way to break a boy's heart; naturally, he said, she wouldn't always be interested in the boys who were interested in her (have you seen my daughter? she's a stunner), and that was okay. The important thing, he explained, was that she always respected a boy's feelings, and if she had to let him down, she should be as kind as possible in the process.

"Teenage boys are a lot more fragile than they look," he confided in her. "Just imagine how you'd want a girl to treat Toby. That's how to handle it."

As advice goes, it remains among the best I've ever heard.

Not long after Bay found out that she had a biological father—when we were frenetically trying to pull together the lawsuit against the hospital for mixing up the babies—I was crossing the driveway and happened to overhear Bay and John talking in her art studio.

She was just finishing up a new piece she'd created by

arranging masking tape on the canvas, then painting over it and removing the tape to reveal a series of brilliant white interconnecting lines and shapes. I'd seen it earlier that morning and couldn't make heads or tails of it. Bay's work, like Bay herself, had a depth that belied the age of the artist. I knew I would come to some understanding of it eventually (or I'd break down and just ask Bay to explain it to me). But this was one of those pieces I'd need to think about for a while.

"Hey," said John, wandering into her studio. He had his hands in his pockets and he looked shy and boyish. "I just wanted to see how you're doing."

"Fine."

I heard his shoes scuffing across the cement floor, I guessed to get a better look at her work. "Nice use of color and line."

(Since "Art" wasn't exactly John's native language, I was impressed.)

"So what I didn't get to tell you the other night," he continued, "is that the lawsuit has nothing to do with you. Your mom and I, we're so lucky to have you in our lives. You make us look at the world differently. Like, like . . . that painting . . ."

Uh oh, I thought. *It was a good call on the line and color, pal, but don't get cocky. One wrong word and you don't get to finish this conversation. . . .*

There was a brief silence in which I suspected he was taking a closer look at the canvas.

"You took the word 'MAN,'" John said with the confidence of a connoisseur, "and somehow turned it into an actual guy and a question mark at the same time."

A guy and a question mark, huh? Go figure. I never would have guessed.

"It's amazing," he went on. "And I have no idea how you came up with that."

"You saw that? The question mark?" Now Bay was the one who was impressed. And judging by her voice, very pleased as well. "I wasn't sure anybody would get it."

"I don't know if anybody would," John said. "But I did."

I felt my throat tighten a little, and I left before the tears began. In just a few words, he'd summed it all up. Not anybody. Him. He was the one who would always see the things she needed him to see, the things other people couldn't (or wouldn't), the things no one but the man who drank tea with her from a tiny cup would ever get. They were connected—not by blood but by something far more magical. He was her hero. And in many ways, maybe now more than ever, she was his.

Sometimes, late at night when I can't sleep, I find myself picturing Bay in an exquisite wedding dress—one utterly of her own choosing. I try not to picture it accessorized with combat boots, but with Bay, you never know. And if that's what she wants, then honestly, it's fine with me. I know she'll look gorgeous no matter what.

And in this picture in my mind, I see my husband, as proud as any father has ever been, walking his little girl down the aisle. But in the next moment my heart goes cold because into this beautiful image creeps a dark-eyed man—a man claiming that he should be the one holding Bay's hand and beaming with pride.

His name is Angelo. And he says that he is the father of the bride.

But he isn't. He can't be. He never kicked a paint-drenched soccer ball. He doesn't know who Danny McMullen is. He wasn't there.

It's his loss.

But it's not his fault.

And that is when I remember that there are still so many questions that as yet remain unanswered and that, although we've come so very far, we still have a long way to go on this wonderful, heart-wrenching journey of ours.

* * *

I will not say much about Angelo except that he is Bay's biological father. He made a brief appearance soon after we discovered the switch.

He also made a lot of mistakes.

When Angelo arrived, Bay seemed to float on air. I think she'd been feeling that she'd gotten the short end of this new blended family. At first, all Regina would reveal about the man who had fathered her daughter was that he had taken off after Daphne went deaf. Since then, his whereabouts had been unknown.

In fairness, when Angelo reappeared, he treated Bay with nothing but love, kindness, and respect. It was hard for John to watch them interact—as hard, I suspect, as it had been for Bay to watch John shoot baskets with Daphne. I felt for John, who was not used to coming in second, or even tying for first. Secretly (and I'm not proud of this) I took just the teeniest bit of satisfaction in watching him muddle through what I had been dealing with since the day Regina moved in. There were times I almost said to him, "See? How do *you* like it?" But I never did.

Angelo, sadly, reverted to type and disappeared again shortly after he arrived. Bay was hurt of course, and confused, but I am happy to say that she wasn't devastated by the departure of the handsome, dark-haired man who, in reality, was and would likely always be more stranger than father.

The thing was, Bay didn't need another father, and she knew it. She had John's love, and she had his name, and she had his constancy.

And all these years later, under a paint-spattered tarp at the back of her garage art studio, she still had an impressive, six-by-six-foot piece of artwork she'd titled *Youth Soccer*.

No kid ever had a better legacy than that.

CHAPTER SEVEN

John and Kathryn Kennish v. Mission Hills General has not
been easy for me.

John wanted to sue, right from the beginning. The hospital was negligent to say the least, and we've all suffered as
a result of this incompetence. John believed the institution
must be held accountable.

The person who would be guiding us through this second phase of our legal pursuits was none other than Harrison's daughter, Amanda Burke, who was a well-known and
highly respected attorney in her own right. Harry (who I
still secretly thought of as Captain Justice) had recom-
mended her, and frankly, I didn't mind that he was bowing
out. I was intimidated by his aggressive style, and although
it had served us well during our search for Daphne, I was
happy this time to have someone who approached things
with a little less zeal. His significantly less blustery daughter
(or, as I couldn't help but think of her, his sidekick, Sub-
poena Girl) was just fine with me.

Maybe that was because I wasn't sure my heart was
even in it. We had found Daphne, and now that we had her,
I was not convinced that having our day in court was going
to bring me any satisfaction. If anything, I worried that
pursuing it further might cause us more pain.

Amanda's first order of business was to direct us to get
Regina to jump on the legal bandwagon.

"The hospital wants this to go away quietly," Amanda explained. "If they settle with you and not her, she's still free to run around town disparaging them."

We told Amanda we could take care of that. Getting the other interested party, the other wronged mother, to join our crusade seemed like an easy enough task. But it wasn't.

At first, Regina told us she'd think about it. John was careful to explain that taking part would cost her nothing; he even pointed out how much she could benefit from the monetary payoff if we won, which, of course, we had every intention of doing.

But Regina remained cagey.

When we approached her the second time, after giving her what we felt was more than enough time to contemplate such a no-brainer, she seemed clearly miffed. She even accused us of being those litigious vulture types who would sue for damages over something as stupid as having hot coffee spilled on them.

I was stunned. How could she possibly compare hot coffee to a missing child?

As she hurried off in the self-righteous huff that became her standard mode of departure, I felt a strange, menacing sensation; the hair was prickling at the nape of my neck and my stomach had gone cold.

"There's something weird there," I said to John, watching this stranger who had raised my child climb into her car and drive away. "I can feel it."

It was more than a hunch. It was equal parts suspicion and intuition, a good old-fashioned gut feeling. At that mo-

ment, I had the overwhelming sense that Regina Vasquez
was lying to us about something.

And as it turns out, I was right.

* * *

Even without Regina in our camp, John wouldn't budge.
He had every intention of soldiering on with the suit, even
when things started to look a lot less open-and-shut than
they had at the beginning. We could have just accepted the
settlement. Or not even bothered; God knows we didn't
need the compensation and, really, it wasn't about the
money anyway. We could have walked away, but John
wanted the hospital to admit they had been remiss, he
wanted them to apologize, and he was determined to see
this through.

We were fighting on the side of the angels, after all. How
could we lose?

But what we didn't have was the ability to see what was
right there in front of us. We were preoccupied with so
many things. There are conversations that echo back to me
even now, reminding me of how naive and trusting we were.
And how our trust had been so thoroughly misplaced.

So yes, we could have taken the money and run, do-
nated it perhaps to a charity that benefits deaf children. But
we didn't. And then one day we were given the news that
there was no longer any money to run with. The hospital
had withdrawn its bid to settle.

And that meant they had something on us. But what
was there to know?

"If they've dug up some 'dark secret' on us, I want to

know what it is!" This was John's reaction upon learning that the hospital's monetary offer was no longer on the table.

I was appalled. "What do they want to hear? That I shoplifted once when I was twelve? That I fall asleep in church?" Frankly, I'd be more concerned about my mother learning of those things than some judge.

My husband looked at me and there was something strange in his expression. It wasn't doubt exactly, but it was close. "You're sure there's nothing bigger?"

I flinched. In nearly twenty years of marriage I'd never seen him look at me like that, and my response was visceral. His faith in me was being challenged. More damage done by the switch. More cartwheels on unsteady ground.

"I'm sure, John," I told him firmly, then hesitated. "And you? Are you 'sure'?"

This implication took him aback, as it had me when he'd used it. "What?"

I kept my voice level. "Any 'dark secrets' I should know about?"

Just saying those words aloud made me queasy, but if he had anything to tell me, I'd rather hear about it now, in his den, than in open court.

His answer did little to reassure me. "None that you should know about."

To this day, I wonder what he meant by that, but at the time, I just couldn't (as Bay might say) "go there."

Ultimately we learned that the hospital's little game of "I've got a secret" had to do with Regina and not us. John approached her about it, and she wrote it off as something pertaining to the DUI convictions she'd accrued back when she was drinking.

If only . . .

John had no choice but to take her at her word, but as "forewarned is forearmed" strategies go, it was a pretty flimsy one; we went into the deposition completely in the dark about what the hospital knew, if anything. I think, right up until the moment I sat down at the conference table, I was still holding out hope that it had all been a bluff, a legal smoke screen to throw us off.

But when I saw the glint in the hospital lawyer's eyes, I knew that this was no bluff.

He knew something, all right.

And so, god damn her, did Regina Vasquez!

* * *

It was unthinkable. Unconscionable! Regina had *known* for thirteen years that she was raising a daughter who was not, rightfully, biologically, or morally hers to raise. She had found out more than a decade earlier that our girls had been switched at birth, and she'd held this secret inside her, like something awful and malignant, and allowed it to grow and fester into the unspeakable situation in which we now found ourselves.

On the ride home from the courthouse, John went so far as to throw out the word "psychopath." I don't know that I necessarily agreed with that term, but there was a certain B-word I definitely thought applied. "Liar"—that was another fitting word. "Kidnapper" wasn't far off the mark either.

John and I confronted her the second we arrived home from the deposition. We did not take a moment to collect our thoughts, or wait for cooler heads to prevail. We assailed the woman, right then and there, and we didn't pull a single punch. The regrettable thing was that Bay and Daphne were there to hear it all. I wish now that we had had the presence of mind to take Regina aside and handle this quietly, in private. But John was incensed; he was livid and out of his mind with the fury over having been played for a fool.

I was angry as well, but I felt something else, too.

What I felt was a crushing sense of betrayal. This woman whom I had begun to think of as a friend had administered a cut as unkind as there had ever been. She'd smiled in my face and stabbed me in the back at the same time.

She'd *known*. She'd known all along and she never said a word.

I felt betrayed. And very, very sad.

It was as though everything I thought I knew, things I thought were indisputable truths, were now being called into question. Was it all an illusion?

I don't know anything anymore, I'd said to John. And truly, that's how I felt.

Regina knew she was caught. To her credit, she didn't deny it.

She told us everything, all of it, from the beginning. And as angry as I was at her, as bewildered and hurt, I recall that in the middle of her explanation I stood up and offered her a tissue. It was a little thing, really, something reflexive—a lifetime of good Midwestern manners doesn't go away just because you happen to be in crisis mode.

But I like to think it was more than that. When I look back on that moment, I realize that even then, even as Regina stood there explaining what she had done, I still could not bring myself to think of her as the enemy.

Kindness trumps all, even if it manifests itself in something as small as a Kleenex.

So she spilled her heart out. She gave us her reason. To John, I know, it sounded more like an excuse.

"I was an alcoholic, unemployed single parent," she told us. "I was broke. I had nothing—nothing but this baby everyone thought was mine, who I loved *so* much. I was such a mess, I was scared if I told the truth, they would've taken one look at me and yanked her away—given both kids to the other family. I looked around at my life and saw how far I had sunk—drunk, alone with a deaf toddler I had no idea how to take care of." Regina wiped at the tears that had begun to well up in her eyes. "And I made a decision. I'd clean myself up. I'd figure it out. I'd get myself back on my feet and *I'd be the best mom I could be.* And I did. I joined AA, I reconnected with my mother, I got it together. And I think I did a pretty good job."

Bay's voice startled me; in the intensity of the moment, I had almost forgotten the girls were there.

"What about me?" she asked. It was part appeal, part accusation. "You knew about me all along and never came for me?"

Oh, how my heart broke to hear her say that! She believed that Regina—her mother—hadn't wanted her! But when Regina turned her tear-filled eyes to Bay, I knew by her expression that nothing could have been further from the truth.

"Oh honey," she said, "I wanted you, of course I wanted you. I even hired a private investigator. He came back with photos and bios of your parents. That's what was in the guitar case. Pictures of you . . . tons of pictures. I followed you constantly. . . ."

This knocked the wind out of me. So my thoughts about Regina passing Bay and me on some department store escalator, or waiting behind us at the grocery checkout, or standing beside us at the swing set in the park had not been so ridiculous after all. She'd been there, watching. She'd seen her little girl.

So why hadn't she given me the chance to see mine?

Bay had a more heartbreaking interpretation. "*I* was your daughter. *Me!*" She glared at Daphne. "Not *her*. And you chose her over me. All those years, you knew I was out there and didn't come for me—"

"Please try to understand—" Regina's voice was filled with regret, with contrition. "I did what I thought was best for you."

"No," Bay countered. "You did what was best for *you*."

I didn't disagree. Regina had had an opportunity to make things right more than a decade ago, and she'd chosen not to. How could I ever come to terms with that?

As Bay bolted from the room, I turned to look at Regina, helplessly clutching the tissue I'd given her, looking guilty, frightened, and alone.

But I still could not bring myself to tell her I understood.

Kindness may come naturally. But forgiveness takes a great deal more effort.

* * *

I went to bed angry that night. Angry and confused.

How in the world had this woman, this mother, kept

such a secret all this time? And how, when we opened our home to her, did she not confess to it?

I couldn't sleep. It was close to dawn when I grabbed my robe, stepped into my slippers, and headed downstairs to make myself a cup of coffee. When it was ready, I took it outside, thinking that witnessing the dawn of a brand-new day might be just the overly symbolic gesture I needed to clear my head.

I was surprised to see Adrianna power-walking up the driveway. She was wearing cross trainers and sweatpants and coming toward me at a good clip for a woman of her age. For a woman of any age, really. I quickly went over the events of the night before and recalled that Regina had said she'd never told Adrianna that she'd known of the switch. Which meant that the woman standing before me now was not technically a co-conspirator.

"Good morning," she said, with a cautious smile. "Couldn't sleep?"

I shook my head. "Coffee?" I offered.

"Love some."

I ducked back into the kitchen, poured a second cup, and came back out to find her already seated in the grouping of patio chairs.

"Thank you," she said, taking the steaming mug.

"I didn't know you went walking in the morning."

"Every day," she replied. "And always right at sunrise. In my old neighborhood it was the safest time of the day. You had to get up early if you wanted to get a jump on the muggers and drug dealers."

I couldn't tell if she was kidding or being serious. I figured it was probably a little of both.

"So I guess you heard . . ." I began. Adrianna nodded, so I went on. "I just don't understand why she would lie."

"Let me tell you a little bit about that point in Regina's life," Adrianna said, gently. She paused to sip her coffee. "And please know that I'm not defending her. I just want you to get a sense of what it was like."

As the sun rose, Regina's mother took me back in time. She told me about how bad Regina's drinking had been, how it had actually created a rift between the two of them, and how volatile Regina and Angelo's relationship had been. Mentally, I reached back through the years to wrap my arms around the three-year-old version of Daphne, who must have watched her mother's self-destruction in wide-eyed terror. The image made me sick to my stomach; but at the same time I took some comfort in the fact that Bay had not had to endure it.

"Imagine the courage it took for her to come to me," Adrianna was saying. "To arrive on my doorstep with her hat in her hand and her heart on her sleeve." She glanced beyond me, to where the first ribbons of sunlight were dappling the rhododendrons, and her eyes were filled with sadness. "She'd said some horrible things to me the last time I'd seen her, and I suppose I'd been pretty rough on her, too. But when she came back, with this little angel in her arms . . . Regina is a proud woman, Kathryn, so you can only imagine what it cost her to come to me and ask for help. She didn't do it for herself, she did it for that little girl."

"And you took her back," I said softly.

Now Adrianna met my eyes. "Of course I did," she whispered, her voice catching. "Just like Bay was your baby . . . Regina was mine."

I felt her words shoot straight to my heart. I tried to picture myself arriving, alone and frightened, on my own mother's doorstep, admitting to her that I was an alcoholic, admitting that I needed help. Would she, like Adrianna, have remembered me as the little girl I once was? Would she have taken me in and helped me find my way?

As if reading my mind, Regina's mother tilted her head and gave me a tiny smile. "What would you have done?" she asked lightly, although the question was a profound one. "And I don't mean what would you have done as Kathryn, a woman who had no addictions, a woman who had, instead of a deadbeat boyfriend, a loving husband and a happy home. Would you have come forward, knowing that there was a very good chance that the one joy you had in the whole world, the little girl you would humble yourself to protect, might be taken from you forever if you did?"

I answered her as honestly as I could: "I don't know."

She nodded. "No, you don't. You can't know. And neither can I. Until we're faced with something like that—no matter how much we like to think we'd do the right thing, or the brave thing, we just don't know."

"It's just going to be so hard for me to forgive her. She kept Daphne from me."

Adrianna traced the rim of her mug with her finger and spoke in a voice that came from somewhere far away. "There were days when she would ask me to sit with Daphne and she'd go out. She wouldn't say where, and always, in the back of my mind, I was afraid she was going to drink again. She'd be gone for hours, and when she would come home—never drunk, never even with the slightest hint of alcohol on her breath—I remember she would look as though she'd just had a piece of her soul taken away from her." Adrianna sighed, and despite the stylish haircut and jogging clothes, I realized she was not a young woman; she'd seen an awful lot in her lifetime, and it hadn't been an easy one.

"I realize now that those were the days when she'd gone to see Bay. To just catch a glimpse, if even from afar, of the little girl she would never know. Can you imagine what it felt like for her every time she had to walk away?"

I leaned back in the patio chair and closed my eyes. I couldn't imagine, and I was glad I'd never had to. When I opened my eyes again, I saw that she had tears in hers.

"Everyone hurts," Adrianna said. "But when it's your child that hurts . . ." Again the older woman's voice broke. "When your child hurts, it is worse than any pain you'll ever bear on your own. Do you know how many times Regina would say, 'Why couldn't it have been me who got sick?' 'Why couldn't I be deaf and not her?' And now I see my child hurting and . . ."

I reached over and held her hand. "It'll be okay," I said softly.

Here we were, two women, two mothers, with only the best interests of two little girls in our hearts.

And suddenly I was remembering a brain teaser book Bay had back when she was in elementary school. It had all the typical riddles in it, like *If a plane crashes on the border of the U.S and Canada, where would they bury survivors?* and *If a rooster lays an egg on a pitched roof . . .* and so on. We kept it in the car to pass the time on long road trips, and I remember one day Bay came across a riddle I'd never heard before.

"Two mothers and two daughters walk into an ice cream shop," she read from the book.

"Are you sure it's not two rabbis and two nuns walk into a bar?" Toby cracked.

"Shush," I said, wondering where he'd been hearing jokes like that. "Go on, Bay."

"Two mothers and two daughters walk into an ice cream shop. They order one chocolate cone, one strawberry cone, and one vanilla cone. And everybody gets their own ice cream."

"That's impossible," John said. "For everyone to get her own cone, they'd have had to order four, not three."

"Maybe they shared," Toby offered.

"Nope," says Bay. "It says they all had their own cone."

"I know!" I said, as the answer—the surprisingly simple answer—arrived like a lightning flash in my mind. "There were only three women ordering ice cream."

"Two mothers and two daughters . . ." Bay said. "That's four."

"Oh, really?" I smiled. "Picture this, if Grandma Bonnie and Bay and I went out for ice cream . . ."

"You'd wind up paying," John joked.

"Probably, yes," I laughed. "But if we did, we would be two mothers—Grandma and me, and two daughters . . . Bay and me."

Bay's face had lit up with understanding. "Because you're not just somebody's mother, you're somebody's daughter, too."

Now the sound of Adrianna's chair scraping on the patio brought me out of my reverie. She stood up and smiled at me.

"You are a good girl, Kathryn," she said, and I drank in the words like cool water on a hot day. "And Bay and Daphne are good girls." Then to my surprise, she leaned down and kissed me on the top of my head. "And Regina is a good girl, too. She lost her way for a while, she's made her mistakes. But she's a good girl."

As I watched Adrianna cross the drive and take the stairs up to the guesthouse, I knew that what she'd said was true. Regina had been in a terrible position, and I can't, with any kind of certainty, say that I wouldn't have done exactly what she did.

I am somebody's mother. And I am somebody's daughter. I am the one who teaches, but I am also the one who still has so much to learn.

Chapter Eight

If there is one overriding question that has been the crucial theme of this journey, that question is *Where do I come from?*

For me personally, I needed to look back and ask myself, *Where did I learn to be who I am? Where did I form the ideas—right or wrong—that have influenced the decisions and choices I've made in my life? Where did John and I begin? Where did we become this couple that has become this family?*

For Regina, it has been about staring into that dark place called alcoholism and knowing that, although that is where she came from, she will never, ever go back.

For Bay, it's been about finding the sense of heritage that evaded her for so long. As much as we've always joked about her lack of athletic ability and her darkly exotic beauty, I know that until now it has been a source of great pain and wonder to her. Maybe because as a painter, Bay has such a powerful appreciation of the visual aspect of the world, she needed to make that connection between her outward appearance and the unique sensibilities of her soul. I understand that she once proudly described herself to Regina as a "Latina artist," and although my Bay has never cared much for labels, this one seemed to suit her just fine.

But for Daphne, the question *Where did I come from?* has a multitude of answers. The most significant, magical, and gratifying element of her journey began long before the switch was revealed. After her illness, thanks to Regina's love and determination, Daphne came from a world of silence and potential loneliness into a world of words spoken in sign, into a proud community of friends and companions who would be there to share her experiences in a way that the hearing people in her life never could. She came from being a fatherless girl into a family with one of the most devoted and loving male role models I could ever imagine. She came from being an only child into a three-sibling household, which includes a big brother who is sworn to look out for her and also to relentlessly torment her every chance he gets.

And she came from East Riverside, a neighborhood where she saw with her own eyes how hard times can lead to bad choices; where dark streets were off limits, and if she ever found herself alone on one, she'd be wise to look over her shoulder more than once and double her pace to get home and lock the door behind her.

Until I met my daughter Daphne, to me East Riverside was a place to avoid at all costs.

Which is why, one day, I decided that I had to go there.

I didn't tell John. I just got in my car and headed north and took the exit as directed by the voice on my GPS, to the place where my daughter grew up.

Was I nervous? Sure. Did I lock the car doors? You bet I did.

And would I have been shocked to see a chalk outline in the shape of a dead body on the sidewalk? Probably not.

Because I was a wealthy woman from the affluent suburbs, and these were the kinds of horror stories we heard about places like East Riverside.

But as I drove the wide boulevards, I was surprised by what I saw. This was not the scene from a *Mad Max* movie I'd envisioned; it was not the demilitarized zone I'd been warned about.

It was a neighborhood in disrepair, certainly. There were a handful of abandoned storefronts with boards across the windows, and the businesses that were still operational had bars on theirs. I saw a fair amount of graffiti, and more than a few teenagers (who should have been in school) wandering the streets looking for trouble.

I saw a homeless man on a park bench, and I saw a very young mother pushing a stroller along a sidewalk bordered by more than a few abandoned cars.

But no shots rang out that had me ducking under the dashboard. And no one rapped on my window offering to sell me drugs or, worse, demanding me at gunpoint to get out of the car and hand over my purse.

The jumpiness I'd felt when I first veered toward the East Riverside exit began to subside.

I saw old women sitting on their front porches, laughing together over coffee. I saw children playing on jungle gyms and storekeepers sweeping the sidewalks in front of their establishments.

I saw life happening, for better and for worse. I saw people doing their jobs, enjoying their families, making the best of the situation into which life, or chance, or choice had put them.

I only panicked when I realized that all my people-watching had caused me to miss the road I was looking for and I'd taken a wrong turn. I consulted my GPS, but since they've yet to work out a system that addresses missing street signs, I realized I was going to have to do this the old-fashioned way.

I was going to have to roll down the window and ask for directions.

I would be lying if I said my stomach wasn't doing backflips when I pulled over to where two men stood on the corner.

They looked to be about my age. Since it was two o'clock on a weekday afternoon, I assumed that they were unemployed. For some reason, this made me even more nervous, as though "out of work" was synonymous with "evil," and then it occurred to me that in our current economy, being unemployed was not necessarily a situation of their own choosing, and that they would probably be happy to rectify that condition if only there were more jobs available.

I hit the button that made the passenger's side window slide downward, and I leaned over the center console to call out, "Excuse me?"

One of the men stepped forward. "Can I help you, lady?"

"I'm lost."

He eyed the BMW and smiled as though to say, "I figured as much."

I gave him the address of the house Regina had rented for the last twelve and a half years. He thought for a minute, then consulted with his friend.

"Two blocks up," he instructed. "Take a right at the stop sign."

I thanked him and drove on.

Minutes later I was pulling up in front of a tidy little ranch-style home. There were bars on the windows, as John had reported after that first night when he'd driven Daphne home—God, was it only months ago? (Honestly, it feels like a lifetime.)

I parked the car and got out. My plan had been to knock on the door and explain that a family member had once lived in this house, and might I please just take a quick look around?

But in the end, I didn't have the guts. I stood on the sidewalk across the street and just took it all in. I admired the tidy flower beds and the freshly painted shutters and the neatly trimmed patch of grass that bordered the front of the house. I thought of the team of professional landscapers that descended on us every other Saturday, and how even with six of them working at once, using their high-powered mowers and industrial trimmers, it took upward of two hours to get the job done.

And yet this tiny plot of grass was every bit as green and cheerful as ours.

Then the front screen door banged open and a little boy of about four or five clambered out onto the stoop. He was laughing as he hopped down the two steps and dashed around to the swing set in the narrow side yard (less grass, more dirt). He wriggled himself onto one of the swing seats and began to pump.

I wanted to call out to him, "Hold on tight," like I used to tell Toby and Bay. Maybe I did say it softly, I don't know. But for close to twenty minutes I just stood there and watched him as he rose higher and higher in a wide arc under a glorious blue sky (as blue as in Mission Hills), and I listened to him giggle with absolute joy at the sensation of swooping toward the sun.

After a while, an older woman, who I assumed was his

grandmother, came outside and stood by the mailbox. Minutes later a school bus chugged to a stop and a girl of about eight or nine bounded down the steps, her Justin Bieber backpack bouncing against her shoulder as she ran to greet her grandmother.

"*Abuela*," she cried. "I got an A on my spelling test."

"*Muy bueno*," *Abuela* replied, catching her in a hug.

Life. Happening.

Just before she turned to lead the little girl into the house, the woman must have sensed me observing them. She turned. Our eyes met.

I smiled. I think I may have even waved.

She nodded at me, smiled cautiously, then called for the little boy to join her and his sister in the house. I don't think she thought I was dangerous, but I was a stranger and I was just standing there, staring at her house.

I would have done the same thing.

When the family had disappeared behind their screen door, I took a moment to memorize the place. In my mind's eye, I saw a tiny, strawberry-blond girl bouncing her first basketball on the cracked pavement of the sidewalk. I saw her getting on the school bus. I saw her learning to ride her bike and playing tag with her friends. All the things I had missed.

I saw Daphne's life. Not the one I could have given her, but the one that she somehow came to have. I ached for what wasn't, and then I smiled for what was.

I had had the great joy and privilege of watching Bay do all those things, and I knew in that I was blessed. But I wanted to have seen Daphne, too. And even though I knew there was no way I could have had them both, that didn't stop me from wanting it. I'm sorry, but when it comes to my children, I'm greedy.

I almost laughed when a police cruiser appeared, moving slowly. The officer gave me a good long look as he drove past, and I knew it was time for me to go.

So I got in my car, found my way back to the highway, and left East Riverside behind me. Not out of fear, or prejudice or snobbery or disgust, but because it was time to go home.

I left because it was not the place that I came from. That didn't make it any better or any worse, it just made it what it was.

And in the end, isn't that what we all want? To find our way home?

CHAPTER NINE

I am sad to report that the Kathryn Tamblyn prom legacy reared its ugly head when the time came for Bay and Daphne to attend the Carlton School for the Deaf formal dance. Unlike me, the girls were not jilted by their boyfriends at the eleventh hour and left to settle for a date of their mother's choosing (although Daphne had a near miss in that regard). Their prom drama happened afterward, and I'm still not clear on the details. All I know for sure is that Bay and Emmett had a huge fight at the dance, and Daphne learned something about her date that was game-changing to their relationship.

I had some drama of my own that night. Due to circumstances beyond my control I was not there to gush over how lovely they looked, or to pose them for those ceremonial pinning-on-the-boutonniere photographs, or to wave them off as they pulled out of the driveway. I did manage to catch up to them at the dance, and I can promise you both of them looked stunning.

But before any of that happened came the question of what they would wear. The minute the date of the prom was announced, I wanted to throw the girls in the car and take them straight downtown to hit every department store and boutique in search of the perfect prom dress. Instead, Regina suggested we at least narrow the playing field by going online, searching the season's best designs and determining which style each girl had in mind. So we gathered in the guesthouse, fired up Daphne's laptop, and began surfing the sites that featured the hottest prom fashions. Daphne was all about feminine elegance; Bay wanted something chic and edgy.

I accepted the cup of coffee Regina had just brewed for me and began to giggle.

"What?" Daphne asked.

"Oh, I was just thinking about my prom gown." I laughed harder, just picturing it.

"Judging by your reaction, it must have been a real winner," Bay deadpanned.

"It was all the rage at the time," I assured her, then smiled at Regina. "Two words," I said. "Gunne Sax."

Regina nearly choked on her sip of coffee. "Oh, Lord. Gunne Sax! Remember all those ruffles?"

"And the lace!" I added.

"The sashes and bows!" Regina shook her head.

"Are we talking about a prom dress here," Bay asked incredulously, "or a baby's bassinette?"

"Wait," said Regina. "Let me guess. Your date wore a powder-blue tux!"

I rolled my eyes, picturing Robbie in that hideous suit. "How did you guess?"

"Because my date wore the same thing."

Now we both cracked up. The girls were looking at us like we were crazy, but for me, it was one of the first genuine "girlfriend" moments Regina and I had shared.

"Actually," I said, putting down my coffee mug and heading toward the door that led to the attic, "I think it's still in a box up here somewhere."

Both girls were out of their seats like rockets.

"This I've gotta see," Daphne signed to Bay.

"Totally," Bay agreed.

We all ducked into the slanting storage attic and began the search. "It'll be in a box marked 'Kathryn's Keepsakes,'" I told them.

Bay found the first box labeled in that manner and dug in. She held up my *Mork & Mindy* lunch box in one hand and my disco roller skates with the neon-pink wheels in the other. "Seriously?" she said.

"What's this?" Daphne asked, tugging a white windbreaker with black trim out of another box.

"My tennis team jacket!" I cried with delight, touching the nylon warm-up lovingly. "From college. Look, I was team captain!" I showed her the black script on the right sleeve: KT. CAPT.

Daphne turned the jacket around and showed Bay the large black letters embroidered in an arc across the back.

Bay scoffed. "You were the Terriers?"

"Woof," said Daphne. It was their turn to crack up.

Then Regina was shouting, "Found it," and there it was. A little wrinkled, a little faded, but there it was. My beautiful lacy, ruffly, peachy-pink Gunne Sax prom dress with its satin sash and high collar.

"It's a freakin' turtleneck!" cried Bay, laughing to the point of tears.

"Did you go to prom in a limo?" Regina joked. "Or a Conestoga wagon?"

Daphne took pity on me. "I like it," she said. "It's . . . vintage!"

I frowned. "Did you just call me vintage?"

"I called the *dress* vintage," Daphne clarified, her eyes dancing. "I called *you* old."

"Very funny!" I snatched the dress away and folded it neatly before returning it to the box.

"You saved everything," Regina remarked, pulling out a handful of chunky plastic cartridges. "Do the eight-track police know about your stash?"

"Okay," said Bay, "before we come across your *Charlie's Angels* fan club membership, I'm out of here."

"Yes," Regina agreed, "too much nostalgia for me. This actually has me thinking about downloading the *Xanadu* soundtrack on my iPod."

"Don't bother, I probably have the eight-track," I offered, grinning.

I had begun to follow them out when I noticed that Daphne was still holding my cherished Terriers windbreaker. A sense of warmth filled me that had nothing to do with the stifling conditions of the attic.

"Would you like that?" I asked her, signing along with my words. "You can have it. I mean, it's still in good shape and besides that . . ." I narrowed my eyes and grinned, "it's vintage."

She gave me her sweetest smile. "I'd love to have it," she said. "Thank you."

I held the door for her, and when she left the attic, I glanced back at the boxes containing the best parts of my childhood.

In another world, I would have taken Daphne to the club for "Toddler Tennis"; I'd have bought her pretty little tennis dresses and matching hair ties, and I'd have taught her the secret of my mighty serve that had brought the Terriers so many victories all those years ago.

But none of that had happened. I think maybe that's why she asked me for my jacket—as a way to make up for those lost moments.

Or maybe she just liked the idea that it was vintage and she'd get some laughs out of the whole Terrier thing.

I didn't know and I didn't care. It was a connection and I'd take it.

Gladly.

* * *

Clearly, "vintage" was "in."

Later that day, Bay came to me in the kitchen and asked, with an utterly straight face, if she could have my Gunne Sax dress.

I did that sitcom thing where I placed my hand on her forehead, implying that she might be fatally ill for even thinking such a thing.

"You want to wear my pink dress to the prom?" I asked.

"Um, yeah, have you met me?" She shook her head. "No, Mother, I do not want to wear it." She looked a little sheepish now. "Actually, I want to cut it up."

That hurt. I loved that dress, or at least I did when I wore it and was named prom queen in it. (Mental note: Go back into attic to look for sash and tiara.) "Why?" I asked.

"I was thinking it could make something with it." Bay's eyes had that twinkle I'd long ago come to recognize as inspiration. "I was thinking I could use the pieces somehow. Maybe on canvas, maybe in some three-dimensional way, you know, like a sculpture."

"Interesting," I said, trying to sound noncommittal, but inside I was thrilled and flattered. I'd abandoned any dreams of Bay wanting to wear my prom dress or wedding gown years ago. That would have been sweet (albeit corny), but hearing that she wanted to use my humble pink Gunne Sax to express herself through her art was by far a bigger payoff.

"It's all yours," I said. "I can't wait to see what you do with it."

"There's more," she said, hesitantly.

I waited.

"Okay, so, remember when Regina told us about . . . you know . . . *knowing*?"

I nodded. Of course she was referring to Regina's revelation about being aware of the switch for thirteen years. She'd even confessed that she'd occasionally follow us to steal a glimpse of Bay. I was getting over that; mostly, I could put it behind me, but being reminded of it still smarted a little.

"She mentioned coming to my piano recital," Bay continued. "She said something about a little blue dress."

Instantly I flashed back to the dress in question. A gorgeous little periwinkle pinafore with pretty puff sleeves, smocking on the bodice, and an oversized satin sash which I looped meticulously into a perfect bow at the back. If lace and frills were genetically transmitted, this dress could have been my prom gown's baby sister.

"Do you still have it?" Bay asked.

I grinned. "Have *you* met *me*?"

"So that's a yes?"

"In the attic," I said on a sigh. "Big box, marked 'Bay's Baby Clothes.'"

"And you don't mind if I use it for the sculpture? If I repurpose it."

She was saying "repurpose" instead of "shred" or "decimate," which was actually thoughtful of her. Again, the image of that dainty little frock, which held so many memories, being torn to pieces stung a little. But the idea of Bay wanting to put two special dresses together—one mine, one hers—to create something heartfelt and original was touching to me.

"I may have an old Members Only jacket of Daddy's up there somewhere," I tossed out. "In case you want to throw a little polyester into the mix."

Bay shook her head. "No thanks. This one is just about us." She grinned and plucked up a pair of heavy-duty scissors out of my utensil drawer.

As she headed off to the guesthouse attic, I closed my eyes and pictured her in that little blue dress, sitting nervously at the baby grand on the stage of the recital. Then I pictured myself standing before the full-length mirror in the bedroom of my childhood, as my mother stood behind me, looping the sash of my prom gown into a perfect bow.

Then I imagined those two dresses inspiring my little girl to create something that would link them and the memories they held forever. I smiled.

I don't know much about art, but I know what I like.

* * *

That night, I kept thinking about two things:

One was Robbie Dennison in that ridiculous blue tux

and the fact that Regina's date had worn the same thing. It was silly, really. If I had a dime for every misguided young man from that era who attended his senior prom in a tuxedo the color of baby booties, I'd . . . well I'd have enough ready cash to pay someone to convert my eight-tracks to CDs. But it was just one more incident where Regina and I had lived a common experience. Apart but, still, utterly connected.

And I also thought about all those boxes in the guesthouse attic. In a very real way, I had managed to pack up my past and put it somewhere where I would always have it; even if I didn't remember exactly where certain items were stowed, they were there. Somewhere. My "memories," in the form of lunch boxes, prom gowns, and team jackets, were saved in boxes, tucked away and stored for safekeeping.

I wondered if I'd saved other kinds of memories, more fleeting, diaphanous ones, not in boxes, but in the back of my mind. Maybe there was something hidden deep in my subconscious, like a box labeled "Keepsakes," that could help me better understand the reality of the switch and all its consequences.

Again, I did not tell John what I was going to do, for fear he would forbid me to do it. Or worse, laugh at me for being gullible. Neither of those options appealed to me so I kept what I was about to attempt to myself.

A few years ago, when my friend Denise was going through her divorce, she took up smoking again. She'd quit back when she was pregnant and had remained nicotine-free for seventeen years, but the stress of the dissolution of her marriage had her lighting up again, and with far too much frequency. Denise is not the sort of girl who would willingly invite yellow teeth and premature wrinkles.

But quitting was simply too difficult on her own. So she went to a hypnotist.

A certified hypnotist, mind you, not some kook with a shabby storefront between a tattoo parlor and the local bounty hunter in a sketchy neighborhood. The guy Denise chose was, according to his ads, a well-respected member of the hypnotism community. Who knew?

The idea of tapping into lost memories intrigued me. If nothing else, I might at least be able to remember which of my friends had borrowed my favorite Williams-Sonoma pizza stone and never returned it.

So I went to the hypnotist's office and told him I wanted to remember, with clarity, a day sixteen years ago. The day my daughter was born. I didn't know if there was a code of ethics in the hypnotism community, and I did not know if, by sitting in the surprisingly handsome leather club chair in the corner of his spacious office, I was entitled to any sort of hypnotist-client privilege, so I decided not to tell him anything about the switch.

When he didn't take out a pocket watch on a chain and begin swinging it before my eyes, chanting, "You are getting verrrry sleepy," I relaxed.

His voice had a deep, resonating timbre as he spoke to me about deep breathing and letting go and walking slowly down a flight of imaginary steps, steps that led to my past.

I can't describe in any real way how it felt to "go under," but I knew when it happened. It was like shaking loose from the laws of gravity and floating within my own life. I felt calm and patient as the memory unfolded in my mind's eye.

The hospital. October. That extra-dazzling autumn light is warming the window of my private room in the maternity ward. John has just left with Toby, who didn't seem overly impressed with his new baby sister. He was wearing OshKosh B'Gosh overalls—denim—and Weebok sneakers, and he brought Baby Bay a present he'd picked out himself downstairs in the hospital gift shop. It is a little pink stuffed pig, nubbly-soft, with a curly tail and a white ribbon around its neck. The nurse allowed him to place it in Bay's portable crib himself. (She still has Piggles, by the way, on a shelf in her room beside her 3-D papier-mâché rendering of Edvard Munch's *The Scream*.)

I sensed that Toby was ready to nap, so I told John to take him home. My husband complied, but not until after he was stopped at the nurse's station and asked to sign autographs for everyone's husband or boyfriend or baseball-obsessed son.

I am alone.

A young nurse comes in and smiles at the addition of the pig to Bay's crib, then she says she's taking her back to the nursery.

Outside of the memory, far away in the hypnotist's leather chair, sixteen years in this memory's future, I am distantly aware of my palms beginning to perspire and my heart pounding. Could I have taken that moment to look just a little more closely at the pretty little baby in the plastic crib? To drink her in enough to know that she was not the little girl who should be receiving such a sweet, brotherly gift? Should I have questioned what I was being told?

No. Because nobody does that. I am not guilty. I am not to blame.

This thought comes to me as a truth that spans both time and consciousness.

Again, I relax, and I watch myself smile at the nurse as she wheels Bay out the door. Then I remember that the doctor wants me to get up and walk. He wants me to get my blood circulating and flex my muscles. That's one of the most amusing aspects of the maternity ward—seeing all these exhausted new mommies pacing the halls. It's like some weird slow-motion race that takes place in pajamas.

I put on the pink robe my mother sent (I received a blue one when Toby was born) and I stand up gingerly, feeling my body object. I recently expelled a six-pound human being from my body, through a very unforgiving portal, after all, and walking is going to be a bit of a challenge.

But it's doctor's orders. So I walk.

I meander slowly, past the nurse's station (smiling to myself as they continue to gush to each other about having just met a real KC Royal) and on toward the waiting lounge. I see a man buying a Snickers from the vending machine, and an elderly couple—grandparents to be, I assume, beaming at each other in anticipation of a new little one to spoil.

I shuffle onward. I turn the corner . . .

And here is what is so bizarre. In the memory, I am surprised, but back in my chair in the hypnotist's inner sanctum, it is as if I already knew.

She was there. She *is* there. *Here.*

Regina! Regina is standing at the broad glass window of the nursery.

I see her as plainly as I saw her just that morning in the driveway, where she asked me if Daphne had left her trigonometry notebook in my kitchen.

Her dark hair is pulled up in a loose knot and she isn't wearing any makeup, but I am startled by how pretty this young woman is. She is still a little heavy around the middle since our deliveries only occurred the day before.

I peer at her from the future, through the eyes of my reminiscence, and I see vividly the smoothness of her not-yet-thirty-year-old face, the fine tautness of the skin on her artist's hands. This stranger I knew would be here in this dream. This memory of a person who will come to share my life in a way I couldn't possibly imagine. I am confusing my tenses. I am here and there at the same time, and the understanding is somewhere in between.

Everything connects, everything is intertwined.

I see her yellow chenille robe and her scuff slippers.

I see that there is no ring on the fourth finger of her left hand.

I see someone who has not been driven to this hospital in her husband's Range Rover, listening to him say, "I told you so" about eating take-out Indian food.

She must feel me staring at her, because she turns away from the glass.

I feel the movement of her head here in the future—or the present—I feel her turning to meet my eyes. And she smiles. Quick, small. A guarded smile, but one that says, "I know exactly how you feel."

"My doctor wants me to walk," I hear myself say.

The words come out of the past, and I imagine them echoing in the hypnotist's office. I spoke to her. Dear God, we actually chatted!

"Mine, too," she says. "The Mommy Marathon."

I laugh. "The Postpartum Parade."

She smiles again. "Boy or girl?"

"Girl." I sigh. I am still giddy about it. "You?"

"Girl."

And then the lactation coach is appearing at Regina's side and ushering her back to her room to begin the process of learning to feed her daughter. Who is my daughter.

And as I watch her go, I hear the voice of the hypnotist crossing the cognitive plane that separates then from now, before from after. He is calling me back, telling me it's time to climb the stairs out of my subconscious. I have unlocked a memory, and I carry it back with me.

It was time to return to the leather chair.

I drifted upward, losing that sense of long ago and drawing back toward right this minute. Then he clapped his hands and I opened my eyes.

"You remembered something," he said. It was not a question. He knew.

I nodded.

As I paid him for his weird but much appreciated services, I made some silly joke about hoping I wouldn't cluck like a chicken every time someone snapped their fingers. He gave me a look that said, "Oh, like I've never heard that one before."

And then I left.

As I drove home, I went back over the memory I'd just stepped out of. There was something profound in what I had just experienced, something that once again goes back to the idea of fate and karma. Regina and I, for whatever reason, were bound. Destined to collide, to interact, to join forces. We inhabited that moment together, and although it seemed so inconsequential at the time, I take great comfort now in knowing that our journey began face-to-face. We hadn't known it, and neither of us actively remembered it—consciously, at any rate—but we'd stepped into this whirlwind having already made a connection.

The robe, the slippers, the ringless finger, the smooth flawless skin—all of that had been tucked away in my memory. In some abstract way, I had been carrying Regina around with me for sixteen years. It was just a matter of finding her.

Like a Gunne Sax dress and an embroidered white windbreaker. You just have to know where to look for them.

Chapter Ten

I have two heroes. Heroines, actually. And I'm proud to say that both of them call me Mom.

Throughout this journey, Bay and Daphne have been the two people who have juggled the most emotions, who've had to face the most profound changes. For Regina and John and me, it has been trying, to say the least, but at no time were our very identities swept away from us. Bay and Daphne, who at sixteen were only just settling in to a sense of self when we discovered the switch, were suddenly forced to ask themselves two questions that would frighten most full-grown adults: Who am I? And where do I belong? The grace and courage with which they have taken on the challenge of answering these questions has amazed me.

This is not to say there weren't some highly tense moments between them.

Part of it, I think, may have been my fault, and that was because I was making the jump from being the mother of two to being the mother of three.

I think about it now and I know that this is a problem all parents have to deal with at some point: striking a balance. The rule is "no playing favorites," and as rules go, it's a good one. But frankly, sometimes it is impossible to find an equitable middle ground. Sometimes, one kid's immediate needs simply outweigh another's. It's a squeaky wheel scenario. And to be honest, there were days, if you asked me which kid was my favorite, I'd have told you, "Well, since Toby broke the dishwasher by trying to steam clean his drumsticks, and then told the babysitter that when Mommy can't find the car keys she uses the S-word, today Bay is my favorite." But there were other times when I would have answered, "Bay just hosted a séance to contact the ghost of her friend's deceased hamster and nearly burned down the house because she forgot to blow out all the candles she lit, so today, Toby is my favorite."

But those would be votes cast in the heat of a very stressful moment. I have always loved both of my two children with equal intensity.

And then we learned about the switch and I suddenly found myself loving three.

I'm sure I made mistakes in those first few weeks. I'm sure Bay must have felt as though all of my attention was focused on Daphne then. And she was probably right. Daphne was not only new to us, she is deaf. We had to learn to speak her language, and to adjust things about our daily lives that until now had been second nature.

But here's the thing. All kids speak their own language. Bay's, as we found out, was "Art with an acerbic accent." Toby's was "Rock 'n' Roll," but he was also fluent in Cleverness, and he is learning to speak Wisdom. All kids are different, and that is the gift they bring us.

Bay never said anything directly about feeling overlooked (and Bay is nothing if not direct), but I think someday, when she's feeling less vulnerable, she'll call me out on it. I won't blame her, either.

And when that happens, I will tell her that I am sorry. I will not defend my mistakes, but I will ask her to try and understand. The equation of our life had a new variable in it, and we had to solve that. Bay was a given; Daphne was as yet an unknown.

And I will tell her that I loved her through it all, even when I seemed to be occupied elsewhere. I will tell her that she was as present in my heart as she ever was. The addition of Daphne to our family did not subtract from my love for Bay.

Lately, I'm happy to say I've noticed a positive shift in the dynamic here at Chez Kennish-Vasquez. Bay told me that she's finally figured out how to classify Daphne when anyone asks her to explain their relationship. "I tell them she's my brother's sister. And when they say, 'Doesn't that make her your sister, too?' I say, "Nope. But I'm her brother's sister, also. Oh, and she's my mother's daughter."

I laughed, even though it sounded a little like a pitch for a Jerry Springer special to me.

And just the other day, I looked out my window and saw Daphne and Bay in the driveway, bent over a giant homemade banner. From where I stood, it looked like teamwork in the making. Later I found out that Daphne had planned to use the painted sign to invite her boyfriend to the Carlton prom.

Daphne was about to discover the advantages to having her brother's super-creative sister in her corner. With Bay's help, Daphne put together a skit that had her dressed as a law enforcement officer arresting this lucky boy and charging him with taking her to the prom.

I understand there were even handcuffs involved. I chose not to ask much after hearing that.

And a few weeks before, Daphne had helped Bay provide Bay's boyfriend, Emmett, with the birthday gift of a lifetime. The girls turned our property into a movie set and filmed a zombie movie, all of the dialogue in which was done in sign language. Regina did hair, John and Toby were extras, Bay starred, and Daphne directed.

And I set up a well-stocked craft services table in my dining room!

It was a meeting of the minds, for all of us. A pooling of skills, a celebration of all our individual talents and gifts.

But of course, this spirit of collaboration wasn't always our mantra. In fact, during the first months of this daring experiment in cohabitation, this place was a veritable powder keg.

Early on there was scuffle, a territorial dispute between Bay and Daphne. Over what? Well, when you consider our circumstances, it probably could have been over anything, but remember, these are teenage girls we're talking about, so you go ahead and take a shot in the dark.

If you guessed boys, you get the prize. But it was inevitable, I suppose.

I was in the process of planning a school fund-raiser, and I was both thrilled and anxious about having Regina and Daphne attend. We were still reeling from the switch, and I was concerned about how people would react when our "news" went public. Aside from my own insecurities about myself as a mother, I was worried about how people would treat Bay when they found out that she wasn't "really" ours.

My concerns for Daphne were less frantic. I knew she would have the advantage of being the pretty new girl, and her sweet, sunny disposition wouldn't hurt either. I worried a little bit about her being deaf. People would be polite, but clumsy, and probably curious. They would struggle to say the right thing and would probably say the wrong one. They might even say "handicapped," and Regina would bristle, but Daphne would be patient and forgiving. Basically, though, I couldn't imagine any of the well-heeled folks in my social circle being anything but courteous, with an eye toward politically correct.

Bay was clearly in the more difficult spot.

Would people suddenly think of her as a stranger despite the fact that she'd lived here all her life? Would she be seen as a pretender to the lifestyle and all that it afforded her? After all this time, would she suddenly be treated like an outsider?

Anyway, with no choice left but to put my fears aside, I invited Daphne and Regina to the fund-raiser bash.

Daphne was excited. "Can I invite my boyfriend?" she asked.

Mention of a significant other took everyone by surprise. But I was able to ask, "What's his name?" and it barely sounded like prying at all. "I'll put him on the guest list."

"Liam," Daphne announced, giddy in that way that only a new boyfriend can make a girl giddy. "Liam Lupo."

This bombshell made Bay the very opposite of giddy. "Wait. . . . *My* Liam?" She sounded as though she'd just been ambushed.

I was with Bay on this one. It didn't make sense. "How are you dating Liam?" I asked Daphne.

Daphne signed and spoke: "I met him when I visited Bay's school."

"Who is Liam?" Regina asked, even more waylaid than I was.

I answered, and Daphne turned to Regina for the ASL interpretation. "Bay's boyfriend."

"What?!" Now it was Daphne's turn to look ambushed. "He never told me he was going out with you."

"We're not," Bay grumbled. "Anymore."

Ambush number three! I turned to my dark-haired daughter. "You broke up with Liam and you didn't tell me?"

"Not the point, Mom," Bay told me, then shifted a look at Daphne. "You're dating someone from my school and you didn't think it was worth mentioning before now?"

The firestorm went back and forth like this for a few minutes, Bay with her own perfected and branded angry teenage sneer, and Daphne's fingers fluttering and flying with the passion and pace of the conversation.

"Look," I cut in, not wanting this to erupt into a full-on battle. "I'm sure we can figure this all out. . . ."

But Bay had yet another surprise up her black lace sleeve. "No, Mom. It's fine. Besides, I'm dating someone else now." She shot Daphne a smug look. "His name's Ty."

"Wait," said Daphne. "My Ty?"

"No," Bay snapped. "*My* Ty."

At this point I really could have used a mai tai. A strong one.

The thing was I knew full well how Bay and Daphne were feeling, because Regina and I were going through the same thing. The boundaries in our new life were hazy at best. We were a living, breathing Venn diagram.

I wanted my daughter and I wanted Regina's daughter and I wanted Regina to quit messing with my frickin' wallpaper. She wanted me to stop imposing my suburban fairy tale on her and her family, and she probably wanted to tell me to take my Birkin bag and shove it where the sun didn't shine.

But none of those things were ever realistic options. And watching the girls work out their differences (which remains an ongoing process) has been not only enlightening but truly heartwarming for me.

Eventually, of course, the Ty/Liam conundrum worked itself out. It was an uneasy truce, a lesson in compromise that served us well because it came up again not long after, when the girls had a similar standoff, this time over Emmett.

As luck would have it, Bay had begun dating Emmett at the same time that Daphne thought her own feelings of friendship for him had blossomed into love. It was a minor romantic altercation, and it was solved soon enough. The real pseudo-sibling-rivalry fireworks came later. And once again, that blasted motorcycle was at the core of things.

Emmett had done something utterly out of character: He got arrested, and slapped with a five-thousand-dollar fine. His only hope for paying it was to sell his beloved bike.

I don't mind saying that would have been perfectly all right with me. But, of course, both Bay and Daphne wanted to rush to Emmett's financial rescue. More to the point, each girl wanted to be the one to rescue him *first*.

But once again, something good came out of it—that is, if you define "good" as having your deaf daughter (at the suggestion of your hearing one) lie to you in an effort to wrangle five grand out of you. And of all things, Daphne chose to lie about losing her hearing aids, which of course was something we would never dream of denying her.

You're wondering where the "good" comes in? Well, I suppose it's all in how you spin it, but for me, the "good" was that when they realized that their individual efforts to assist Emmett were falling short, they forged a united front. This was the first time Bay and Daphne were willing to work together toward a common goal. Their methods may have been on the sketchy side, but deep down, I think their motive was sincere. And they recognized that together, they could accomplish more than they ever could by taking rival stands.

Bay and Daphne acted in tandem to help someone they both cared about very much. They put aside their own differences to bail out (unfortunately, in this case literally) a friend.

I think this is a lesson Regina and I, as dueling moms, will do well to emulate.

Because as sisterly behavior goes, that's about as good as it gets!

Let me be clear. I know that Bay and Daphne aren't blood sisters. Strictly speaking, they aren't even stepsisters. But I like to think of it like this (with my apologies to Donny and Marie Osmond): Daphne is a little bit Bay, and Bay is a little bit Daphne. They walked in each other's shoes without even knowing it. They borrowed each other's history while that history was still in the making. They were each other's warm-up band. And yet they are both delightfully individual and independent.

I feel blessed to have been given more than I ever wanted— to be a part of this bittersweet paradox. My two girls are sharing a most unique evolution. One which very few people will ever be able to comprehend. They are bound. They are connected. And although they may not realize it yet, they are on their way to being friends.

EPILOGUE

So we sally forth, we Kennishes and Vasquezes. We carry on. If someone asked us all, separately, to describe the process, to wax metaphoric on the events of the last year, surely they'd come away with a mixed bag.

Daphne and I might call upon our love of cooking and liken our family to a terrifically complex recipe in which many different flavors are simmering together to produce a one-of-a-kind pièce de résistance.

Bay and Regina, our gifted Latina artists, would surely describe us as a mixed-media masterpiece, a collision of materials and a blending of colors and textures. The most important thing, though, is that the meaning behind this family portrait is always open for interpretation. We are unpredictable, like performance art.

John would go with something sports-related—he'd compare our ever-improving team dynamic to a triple play executed with exquisite timing. Then he'd go slightly off topic to tell you all about the 1985 World Series, the "I-70 Showdown" in which the Royals defeated the Cardinals (just nod and smile, that's what we do).

And Toby would compare us to a symphony, slightly out of tune, but ambitious, with a thousand different melodies, contributed by instruments of every variety. Or maybe he'd define us in terms of the lyrics of some Counting Crows song.

And all of these interpretations would be accurate. Because we see things, always, through the filter of who we are. We absorb the world and make sense of it on our own terms. The conclusion is the same, even if the paths we take to get there are not.

The other day, while I was loading the dishwasher, my husband came up behind me and wrapped his arms around me. We had all just finished dinner—the six of us. I made a big Italian meal using a recipe passed down from my grandmother, the one I'd always credited for Bay's dark hair and fiery personality. I was arranging the silverware in the basket and trying to fit all six drinking glasses on the top shelf in a way that wouldn't cause them to chip.

"I'm proud of you," he said.

I laughed. "Why? Because I always remember to rinse the stuck-on spaghetti sauce from the dinner plates before I put them in the dishwasher?"

"Well, that, too. But I was talking about the book. You're doing something very unselfish, Kathryn. You're helping people."

I would like to tell you he stuck around to help me finish wrapping the leftover garlic bread in tinfoil, but that would be a fabrication. He grabbed himself an anisette-flavored biscotti and headed off to his den to go over the papers our newest lawyer had sent over.

Because that part of this journey continues still. The lawsuit is an ongoing concern, and I don't know when, if ever, it will come to fruition. Unfortunately, I inadvertently set us back a bit when I tracked down the star witness—a nurse named Brizia, who was prepared to swear under oath that on the day the girls were born she'd been forced by her superiors to work forty-eight hours straight, to the point of exhaustion. We are asserting that this is the reason for the mistake that resulted in the switch. I gave this nurse a large sum of money.

If you've come with me this far, then I'm confident you know me well enough to understand that this was not a bribe. I had discovered that Brizia, in return for electing to testify on our behalf, had been fired from the hospital. So I gave her the money not as a plaintiff to a corroborating witness, but as one mother to another. I gave it to her because I didn't want her and her children to suffer because she was doing the right thing.

So the lawsuit is just one more indefinite in our universe at the moment. One more outcome we await. The details and specifics seem to change daily. But then, so do we.

Several months ago, I set out to write a book that I thought would be helpful to anyone who ever faced the nightmare of learning that their child had been switched at birth. I wanted to write a book that was part memoir, part how-to, that might provide insight and advice. I thought my story could help guide parents of switched children through the twists and turns and heartaches of their "lightning strike" situation.

But if this is a book exclusively for them, I hope I never sell a single copy. Because as Regina said when she told us about waiting out Daphne's meningitis, "I wouldn't wish that on any parent." It is my dearest wish that never again will someone require such a reference tool as this one.

And yet, as I reviewed what I'd recorded here, as I reread my own thoughts and reflections (because I was curious to see if I'd pulled it off, and also because my editor said I had to), I realized that this was not merely a book about a hospital mix-up. This was not *What to Expect When You're Expecting a DNA Test* or *Switched at Birth for Dummies*. It's about much more than that. It's about fortitude and forgiveness. It's about ordinary people in extraordinary circumstances. It's about embracing the unexpected and making it work. It's about family and how that word defies definition.

So this is a book for anyone who is part of an "unconventional" family. Stepmothers and stepfathers, stepsiblings, foster children—anyone who arrives a little late to that party known as "the conventional family." It's about finding your place at the table and knowing there will always be enough to fill your plate.

It's for children who have been adopted and for the wonderful, wonderful people who become their mothers and fathers. I believe that God guides the hands of adoptive parents; He leads them to the children they are meant to love. It is the purest form of reciprocity—hearts in need of one another finding their way home. Adoption is nothing short of magical. It is a different path, as I say, but it leads to the same place, to the right place, and that place is family.

And it is a book for anyone who has a child who is different. Our daughter is deaf. She is not broken or defective or strange or inferior. She just can't hear. But she can communicate and she can laugh and she can bake a batch of butterscotch brownies that will knock your socks off. She can date and she can dance and she can sink free throws and ace biology exams; and she can torture her big brother (which, really, he totally has coming to him).

And she can love. Boy, can that kid love.

And this is a book about how she came into my life and made *me* different, made me better than I was before.

This is a book for kids like my darling, darling Bay, who touches your life with her beautiful vision and shows you a world you could never have imagined on your own. She, too, is a kid who loves with all of her heart and soul. She makes me laugh. She is the little girl whom the universe allowed me to raise.

Every day I am thankful.

This book is about fortitude and forgiveness and how there is no way to know what's coming around the next bend, or off the next highway exit.

And it's about life.

Happening.